UNITE THE PARTY

ANTONY SOEHNER

5 Prince Publishing

UNITE THE PARTY

Antony Soehner

5 PRINCE PUBLISHING & BOOKS, LLC

PO Box 971 Golden, CO 80402-0971

www.5PrinceBooks.com

Digital ISBN: 978-1-63112-220-0

Print ISBN: 978-1-63112-219-4

UNITE THE PARTY. Antony Soehner

Published by 5 Prince Publishing

Cover Credit: Joshua Stolte

First Edition 2018

5 PRINCE PUBLISHING AND BOOKS, LLC.

To Julie,

*For believing in all my crazy
aspirations no matter how big.*

Where ever you are, I hope I still make you proud.

ACKNOWLEDGMENTS

A big thank you to my friend and mentor Joshua Stolte for training me in the fine art of being a geek and for creating another beautiful piece of artwork for my books.

To my friends and family, without whom none of this would be possible! Your support means the world to me!

OTHER TITLES BY

ANTONY SOEHNER

Gather The Party

UNITE THE PARTY

Antony Soehner

ONE

MANY GATHERINGS

I STARED OUT THE WINDSHIELD THE ENTIRE DRIVE. NEVER looking off at the signs and billboards on the side of the road, only occasionally reaching down to my phone to hit the next track button. I've had a recent obsession with listening to Elton John.

Mom and I have been cleaning the house lately, and we came across her stash of old cassette tapes and cd books of music from when she and my dad were dating. Elton John, Lionel Richie, Eminem, Tupac, Meatloaf, Queensryche, David Bowie, Bruce Springsteen. The list goes on and on. I've come to appreciate all of them.

They've been great to have these past couple months, with everything in my life changing: getting my license and fixing up dad's old car. Mom picking up a second job and cutting hair in the basement again. Jake returning from deployment and retiring from the military. Ben and his mom fighting his dad in court for custody rights after his dad showed back up. Liam picking up a job working with Daryl's mom. Laura went back to school and getting a prestigious kitchen job as a sous chef. And Daryl spending countless hours at school doing college prep and working on his auditions for all the music programs he's looking at. Even though that's still years away.

But all these old tapes and cd's seem to keep me grounded to what things once were. And remind me where things will go.

Lucky for me though, I've got Spotify so I don't have to lug all those boxes in my car to listen to them. I opened my phone and scrolled through the *Number Ones* album by Elton John. I clicked on *Saturday Night's Alright* at the bottom and turned it up.

I started getting into my head space, like I always do on the drive to Liam's. It's harder now to fully prep since I started driving myself. I can't check my sheet while I drive. But it also helps me memorize my stats just a bit more.

"Adrik Frostbeard," I started saying to myself. "Level thirteen barbarian dwarf. A hundred and twenty-five hit points," I listed off. "Nineteen strength," I stopped and chuckled a little to myself. "Charisma... Nine."

I still get a laugh out of my broad, buff, and awkward dwarf version of me. I still can't see me ever being able to wield an axe like Adrik. But at least I can usually talk my way out of pretty bad situations.

The song began its final piano riff as I reached the gravel driveway that led to Liam's house. As I pulled up and put the car in park, I sat and let the song finish out before removing the auxiliary cord. I killed the engine, unbuckled my seatbelt, and sat there for a minute. When I was younger, I always dreamed about being able to drive to Liam's on Fridays, although I'm starting to miss having Mom drive me.

I popped my door open, hopped out, and lifted the back to grab my bag out of the trunk. Throwing the bag over my shoulder, I slammed the trunk shut, and walked to the door.

I could hear someone's phone go off through the open window as I approached the front door and set off the motion sensor doorbell. And before I could even make it up the ramp to the porch, there stood Liam in the open doorway.

"Wow, expecting, much?" I teased him as I pushed past him into the house.

"Oh, can it," he responded giving me a shove. "You're the one who has nothing better to do on a Friday night than play games at my house."

I smiled and shook my head. "Isn't that a good thing?" I said, walking further into the house towards the kitchen. "So where is he?"

"Who?" Liam asked.

"Your uncle, numbnuts," I shook my head again. "The only reason I like coming."

"Oh, cut the bullcrap," he said punching the back of my shoulder. "You know the real reason is so you can keep that fantasy in your head that Laura will still be available and fall in love with you over whatever idea of heroism you can attempt in this fantasy game we've been playing for years. All in the hopes that one day you will both get married and raise geeky children in your own image," Liam analyzed.

I rolled my eyes at him, but he wasn't totally wrong. I really do like coming to see Laura. Not that I think we're going to get married or anything he just said. But I won't deny that the thought hasn't crossed my mind before. I can't admit that out loud.

"Oh, shut it," I responded. "Where's he at?" I asked again.

Liam rolled his eyes at me this time and smiled. "He went to get more soda. You drank through most of it last week, remember?"

"Hey man, it was really dry last week,"

"Either way, he's at the store."

"Works for me, gives me time to hide this again," I said, reaching into my pocket.

"You didn't," Liam groaned.

"I didn't do a thing," I smiled at him. I pulled out a folded wad of cash from my pocket. "Now turn around. I don't want you seeing where I'm hiding this." I pointed at him and moved my finger in a circle directing him to turn away. Once he wasn't looking, I spun around and opened the dish cabinet. I took the cash and put it under a plate in the middle of the stack.

"Are you done yet?" Liam asked. "You know he doesn't spend any of the money you guys leave him, right?"

"Well then what's he doing with it? Saving it for us all to go to college or something?" I asked. "Because he could use that money for a ton of better things. Lord knows you and I aren't getting into any college," I joked.

Liam's phone started to chime again, alerting us someone was at the door.

We both ran over to the door and Liam opened it. And there on the porch stood my man Wade!

"Hey, hey, little dudes! What's crackin'?" Wade asked.

"What's going on, Wade? How's work been tonight?" I responded.

"Ah, you know how it is man, party full of drunk people here, stoned gamer kids there, over-stressed parents trying to feed the sleepover they didn't plan for. Pretty casual. What about you guys? What went down last week?" he asked, raising his eyebrow in curiosity.

"Oh man, you wouldn't believe what we did!" Liam began excitedly. "We've still been searching for Elfi and whatever the hell is going on with this Death's Hand group, but we made it to Dracomear, finally, to get some answers. We had to sneak in. They don't like outsiders within their walls. So I'm praying to the Raven Queen we survive this." Liam stopped and drew in the missing oxygen that wasn't reaching his brain after rambling through all that. "But if all goes well tonight, we should be closer to learning who this Greg guy is."

"Who's Greg?" Wade asked, raising both his eyebrows now.

"Oh man, who isn't Greg?" I responded. "He keeps coming up in everything. It all seems to tie back to him. Reita, Death's Hand, Elfi, The Order of Melora, everything!"

"That's brutal, dude!" Wade laughed. "What's the plan for tonight? What are you doing in Dracomear?"

"Well according to Torinn, there are answers in the ancient library there. We're searching for anything. Tomes on all of it," Liam added. "We're at a point where anything will help."

"Well how about a little of this?" Wade said as he popped open the red carrying case and slid out seven large pizzas. "I got one cheese, one pepperoni, one sausage, one hawaiian," he paused. "And tell Laura that's totally gross, pineapple on pizza is a sin!" He joked. "One veggie for the vet, meat lover for the game master, and of course, the Jack special," he finished as he slid out all the pizzas and handed them to us.

"Are we your largest order?" Liam asked as he took the pizzas.

"Ya know the crazy thing is, you're my second largest tonight. We have a huge order for late tonight. It's either a frat party or a really exciting business party, but they ordered two of everything. Tonight is gonna pay Kurtis' rent for the restaurant this month." Wade laughed. "Which reminds me, I've got something in my car for you guys," he said as he turned down the ramp and ran back to his car.

He came back up the drive seconds later carrying a paper bag that was wet on the bottom.

"What's that?" Liam asked puzzled.

"Oh man, are you guys gonna freak," Wade said with a smile. He handed me the bag and I took a look inside. There were plastic containers that were fogged over with a thick layer of condensation to the point I couldn't see in them. Under that were two plastic white tubs that were also dripping wet. But that explains why the bag was wet.

"What's all this?" I asked through my confused laughter.

"Well Kurtis has been expanding our place beyond just making pizza lately. He's working on rebranding as a pizzeria and delicatessen. So he sent me with a bag of items he wants you guys to try and tell him what you think!" Wade responded excitedly. "In the two plastic containers are cannolis, rainbow cookies, and pizzelles. And the white tubs are spumoni. That's why the bag is wet. They were frozen, that's why I was racing over here to get to you guys. So get that in a fridge soon. Or eat it all now."

"Wade, this is too much man. Can we send you with some money or something?" Liam asked. "I know Uncle Matt isn't gonna be okay with all this for free."

"Sorry dude, Kurtis specifically said no money on this one. You guys spend so much with us each week and have been for years. He says it's the least he could do." Wade smiled.

"Well here then," I said as I tucked my hand into my pocket and grabbed the twenty bucks my mom gave me and handed it to him. "Your delivery tip, if you wanna share it with him that's up to you. Or keep it, either way you guys deserve it."

He reached out and took the twenty bucks. "Man you guys are always the coolest delivery I make every week." His smile widened. "So, same time next week my dudes?" he asked, shooting us finger guns.

"Oh for sure," Liam and I responded together. He gave his signature over the head, hang loose hand symbol, Breakfast Club ending walk away. Liam and I laughed and returned the hand signal before closing the door.

"Ok, before you make a mess," Liam said turning to me. "Go

throw that stuff into the freezer in the garage before it melts all over the place."

"I'll go to the garage with them..." I smirked. "But no promises that it ends up in the freezer." I laughed manically.

"Well if you're gonna be your normal, fat self," Liam scowled with a smile. "At least save me a cannoli."

I just smiled and walked towards the garage.

I opened the door from the kitchen into the laundry room and went in and past the washing machine that was aggressively shaking and rumbling. I crossed the room and opened the other door that lead into the garage. I walked down the makeshift wooden ramp made of multiple boards of plywood.

Mr. R's garage had a thick odor of paint and lacquer. This was where his workshop was hidden. There were no cars or bikes in the garage. No camping or Christmas gear. In fact, unlike all the garages I've ever seen, it was spotless. There were shelves full of painted statues and figures. Up against the wall sat his painting station. A large workbench with rows on top of rows of small paint containers. Cups full of brushes, all different sizes and bristle shapes. In front of his bench sat a tall stool with a fabric strap handle over it hanging from the rafter above.

On his bench he had a what looked like a gruesome looking troll creature sitting in front of a blowing fan.

I walked around looking at his collection of statues. He had everything. There were statues of Batman and Robin, Gandalf and the dwarves, Bilbo and Frodo. Some statues depicted scenes from movies and comic books while some were scenes from his imagination. There was one that I kept getting drawn back to. It was hidden up high on the top shelf. I reached up and pulled it down to look at it.

When I pulled it down, a piece of paper fell from under it. I bent down to pick it up, setting the paper bag down. I turned the paper over, and saw a photo. It was a picture of the moment the statue is based on. It was of my dad and Mr. R when they were younger. I turned it over and saw there was writing on the back of the picture.

Matt and Travis, D&D night
July 15th 20—

The date was smudged at the end. Maybe water damage or something. This was taken back when all our families hung out constantly. Both my parents, Jake, Ben and Laura's mom, Laura's dad, Liam's parents and his uncle with his fiancée.

I've heard the stories from when they were younger. The all-nighter game nights, going to Kurtis' pizza shop after getting crazy drunk, all the shenanigans people in their early twenties do.

I could feel a slight knot building in the back of my throat. Looking between the picture and the detailed statue of my father and a younger Mr. R.

"You know, now that I see it, you look a lot like him."

I jumped and spun around. Clutching the statue a little tighter in my hand. It was Mr. R sitting in his wheelchair. He'd snuck up behind me.

"You both have the same smile. It's kinda spooky," he laughed. "You alright?"

I became aware of the tears now trickling down my face. "W —what? Oh, yeah. Yeah I'm all good," I sniffed, wiping my tears off my cheek. "All good."

"It's okay to cry, bud," Mr. R assured me. He reached out and pulled me down into a hug. "I miss him too. Not a week goes by I don't. Every day I wish I could go back and save him. But it's been getting easier. Because each week I get to hang with all you kids and relive a life that seems so far gone."

I could now feel the flow of tears begin to stream out of my eyes and soak his shoulder.

"Now, don't tell your mom I told you this." He moved me back to my standing position in front of him. "But that was the night your dad and I convinced Jake to drink for the first time—and probably the last." He laughed through the catch in his voice. "He took his first few shots really fast and ended up throwing up all over your mom. And boy she was not happy about it." He chuckled as he took the picture and examined it. "I tell ya, Jack, I'd give everything to have your dad play with us again. But now, I get an even better experience that I have you here. His doppelganger, his clone—his son. But, you also have some of your mom in you to balance out. Which believe me when I say, that's a really good thing."

Mr. R turned his chair around toward the door. "Now set those silly memories back on the shelf and throw that bag in the freezer before it melts." He smiled as he opened the door and wheeled into the house.

I turned and put the statue with the picture back where I found them. I picked up the bag, which was now completely falling apart, and quickly ran it over to the freezer, then I hurried back into the house.

As I made my way back through the laundry room and into the kitchen, I heard both Liam's and his uncle's phone go off with the doorbell alert again. I went and answered the door to Ben and Laura. Laura's expression said it all.

"You let Ben drive didn't you?" I asked, chuckling at her expression of anger and fear.

"How could you tell?" Laura asked, brushing her hair down. "Is it the face of almost dying? The windblown hair? Or the streaks of tears across my face?" She didn't seem as playful about this as I was hoping.

"Calm down," Ben moaned. "It wasn't even my fault. He

started going before the light even changed. It turned red as we were in the intersection. You're just lucky I'm as skilled a driver as I am or you wouldn't have a car left!" He rolled his eyes. "Anyways, what's up? Are we the last ones again?"

"Actually," I heard Liam say as he came into the front room, "Daryl and Jake aren't here yet."

And almost like the stars aligned, a large black truck pulled into the driveway, and out got the two brothers.

"Never mind, everyone's here," Liam corrected himself.

"Well, I guess you were right D," Jake said as he walked up the path. "We were late. My bad." He reached into his pocket and pulled out a five dollar bill and handed it over to his brother.

"Thank you," Daryl sang as he took the money. "It's been a pleasure doing business with you." He smiled as he joined the group on the porch.

"Well, quit lollygagging and get in here," Liam said, dragging me out of the doorway. "Pizza's gonna get cold!"

We wandered into the kitchen and Liam started flipping open pizza boxes and putting out plates.

"By the way, Laura," Liam said not looking up from his piles of plates he was counting. "Wade says you're gross for putting pineapple on your pizza."

"Eh, who cares, they made it and I'm gonna eat it. What can he do about it?" she responded. "He's not the first, and won't be the last one to tell me his opinion on pizza," she said as she grabbed a plate and pulled a slice from the pie. She didn't even let it hit the plate before she started eating it.

"Easy there, slick," Ben said to his sister. "That'll go to your thighs," He laughed.

She set the pizza down on the plate and cocked her fist in the air, jumping at Ben. He quickly jumped away and threw me between them.

"Hey!" I shouted. "I'm not playing human shield in this.

You made a weight comment to a woman, now get out here, be a man, and take your punishment," I said as I pulled him out from behind me and threw him at Laura.

"Thanks, Jack," She smiled, and then proceeded to punch her brother right in the shoulder. He spun around to face me, holding his shoulder in pain.

"And for using me as a meat shield," I said to him before punching him in his other shoulder.

"Dude!" Ben shouted at me. I just shrugged.

"Hey, you deserve it," Laura chuckled.

I moved away from the two of them and grabbed my own pizza. I noticed my bag was still on my back when I leaned against the counter. I looked around at everyone and smiled a little. It was nice to think that we have our own group to cause shenanigans with. And it's a mix of blood relations and friend-ships. But I guess you could call this a family.

Gross. That was a real sappy thought.

"So, Jake," Liam asked across the room. "You've been out of the military for quite a while now. How's civilian life treating you?"

"Oh, uhh," he hummed, as he was in the midst of shoving a slice in his mouth. He took a second to chew. Putting his finger up before swallowing. "It's been alright. It's nice to have the ability to come home and get a full-time job with no problem. I'm loving getting to play with you guys each week. Speaking of which, I got a little something you guys are gonna like," he said as he rolled up the sleeve on his right arm. Under the sleeve he showed us a fresh-ish tattoo of a two dimensional twenty sided die inked into his arm, inside the middle triangle was a number seven.

"Why a seven?" Ben asked.

"Well there are seven of us." He smiled looking back at his tattoo. "Figured you guys would wanna see that."

"Dude," Laura said. "That's awesome." She turned around and lifted the hair off the back of her neck. And there on the bend of her neck was the same two dimensional d20. But it was blank. "We kinda had the same idea!"

"When did you do that?" Ben asked concerned.

"A couple months ago," She responded, putting her hair back. "And mom doesn't know, so I would like to keep it that way," she said to Ben with a stern look.

He mimed zipping his lips and handing her the key.

"Thank you," she said, accepting the imaginary key.

"Well I think that it's pretty awesome." I piped up.

"Of course you do," Liam mumbled under his breath. I promptly jabbed my elbow deep into his ribs, causing him to groan.

"Thanks, Jack," Laura chuckled giving me a wink. And like it always happens, my knees turned to jelly and almost gave out.

Why? Why did my knees always go weak? Every time she winks at me, talks to me, looks at me! That toothy smile. That soft voice. Those beautiful eyes. You could lose yourself in those eyes. I know I have. But there's more to her than her beautiful looks, so much more. Something about her intimidates you. Not like you stand there in fear she'll hurt you. But that she is powerful. Behind that soft voice, there's force. She could convince both a genius and a meat head to hold hands and think they were married, just by saying it. And that... that power in her voice. That's what gets me every time. She's just amazing, and I can't wait until she's mine...

"You okay there, Jackie?" I heard Laura interrupt my thoughts.

"W—what? Oh yeah, yeah I'm great! Why?" I asked, coming back into my head. Little did I notice that everyone had left Laura and I alone in the kitchen.

"Dreaming again?" she asked smiling. There they went again. My knees.

"Pfft," I scoffed. "No way. I—I was thinking—"

"About us again?" She chuckled.

"W—w—what are you talking about?" I stuttered. "I've never done that," I lied. I could feel the blood rushing to my face.

"Sure, whatever you say." She winked again. "Whenever you're done fantasizing about real life, we're waiting to fantasize in another world." She smiled walking away into the other room.

I sat there watching her walk away before shaking my head aggressively and smacking my cheeks a few times. "Get over yourself! Stop it, you bum!" I said to myself. "It'll never happen! You know that!" I shook my head again and pushed off the counter. My bag dropped off the counter and hit my back hard enough to knock me forward a few steps. I grabbed a plate, snagged some more pizza, took a root-beer from the fridge, and darted into the game room.

TWO
SHADOW OF THE RECAP

"DUDE, FINALLY!" DARYL SHOUTED AS I RAN THROUGH THE doorway. "How hard is it to scrape your jaw up off the floor?" He jolted in his seat and glared at Ben before pulling his chair back under the table.

I didn't even bother responding. I put my food and soda down on the table and took my bag off my back and began to rifle through it. I pulled out my binder, manuals, pencils, and dice bag. I set them with a thud on the table next to my food, took my seat, and looked around the table.

Everyone was looking down at their phones. Scrolling with their thumbs. Double tapping this and swiping that. I looked to Mr. R and realized his spot was empty.

"Where's he at?" I asked pointing at the empty Dungeon Master's spot.

"Well, what'd you expect?" Liam chimed not looking up from his phone. "You were taking forever, his bladder is getting older, and he drank a whole can of soda while you were in there gawking at Laura."

He jolted like Daryl had, but promptly returned the favor to

Ben with a swift punch to the shoulder. Without looking away from his screen.

"What the hell, man?" Ben whined, rubbing his shoulder.

"If you're gonna kick someone, don't be a little bitch when they hit back—"

"Eh-hem," Mr. R coughed as he wheeled into the room.

"Sorry for calling you a—" Liam stopped as his Uncle raised his eyebrow. "Sorry for calling you that word." he sighed.

"Better," Mr. R smiled as he moved into his spot at the table. He took the laptop from his lap and placed it on the table, plugging in the HDMI cable. The TV in the table gave its usual chime and turned on, showing the picture of the massive library from the last session.

Massive? No! Gargantuan bookcases that ran for miles in this place. Each one filled and overflowing. So many books and scrolls that there were tall stacks of tomes and parchment across the floor too.

"Let's do the rundown," Mr. R said followed by a heavy throat clear. Everyone put their phones away. Some on the table, some in their bags. We all closed our eyes. "Let's start to my left, Gimble?"

"Ah, I am here my friend. Violin at the ready!" Jake replied.

"And Lerissa?" Mr. R asked.

"I'm always here, ready to finally learn what the hell is going on." Laura said.

"Torinn?"

"Y—y—yes!" Daryl stuttered as he transitioned into his character's voice. "I am still here and pray to Pelor in hopes of being here for a bit longer."

"May the gods be in your favor," Mr. R responded. "And Rolen? How goes it?"

"Another day, another adventure," Ben joked, "Another day closer to becoming the powerful druid I'm supposed to be."

"I love it." Mr. R chuckled. "Ront?"

"Hmph," Liam exhaled. "I'm still alive so there's that."

"And Adrik?"

"Aye!" I cheered. "My hammer and I are here to slay."

"Then if everyone's comfortable, let's begin." Mr. R said.

One by one we each opened our eyes and lifted our heads. Daryl began rolling the few d20's he had pulled out from his case, Liam rolled his new black dice to 'train' them, and Jake was admiring the blue sparkle in his. I moved my gaze over to the left at Laura.

I almost fell off my chair when she locked eyes with me. Her eyes were a scary yellow and red mixed color. Just like Anakin's eyes in the end of Revenge of the Sith.

I signed to her, *What did you do?*

My Eyes? she signed back.

Yeah!

They're my new contacts I ordered. You like? She smiled at me.

It was a little weird, but something about the scary eyes made her even more attractive!

Yeah, they're cool. I signed, followed with a thumbs up.

They're the same kind Hayden Christensen had in Star Wars—

If you guys don't mind. Daryl interrupted, motioning at Mr. R.

Sorry. Laura and I signed together.

"As we last left off, the six of you had been following the trail of clues concerning the disappearance of your lost companion, Elfi, and the mystery of the cult, Death's Hand," Mr. R began to recollect. "You scoured through the continent of Myciya. Searching in the dark market in Shadestone. Revisiting Tal'ireald and Faria but to no avail. Until Ront stumbled upon a clue that has led you here to the Grand Library of Dracomear, the home country of your companion, Torinn. After being denied entrance to the massive library, you all decided to sneak your way in, almost getting caught. Now you all hide in the Grand Library in hopes of finding something on the evil cult of death."

"Well, you guys," Torinn said. "Where do we start?"

"I wanna keep searching the library," Lerissa responded. "There has to be something useful here."

"Give me an investigation check," Mr. R instructed. Laura took her d20, gave it a good shake and let it go onto the table top.

"Twenty-two," she said, scanning her character sheet.

"You go looking up and down aisles of books and scrolls, scanning through a few here and there. Until you come across one particular book—" He paused. He clicked his keyboard and the screen changed to an image of a leather-bound book. "You pick up this book off the top of a stack on the floor. Looking at the cover, you notice a familiar symbol." He clicked the keyboard again and there it was! The symbol of Death's Hand was embossed in the leather cover. "You feel an arcane energy flow through you, chilling you to the bone as you stare at the red gemstones embedded in the eyes of the raven symbol."

"I run my fingers over the symbol, and then I want to cast dispel magic," Lerissa said.

"As the chills run down your arm, you channel your energy and begin to focus on dispelling the magic presence of this book. As you feel the warmth surging down your arm and into the leather cover, you watch as a dim burst of light surrounds the tome. Like blowing dust off an old box, a shadowy, dark, and ethereal magic blasts off the cover," Mr. R said, mimicking the magic effects using one of his manuals. "That feeling of cold and darkness has vanished."

"I open the book to the first page," Lerissa said.

"As you open to the very first page, you see this written in Abyssal," Mr. R sat up and handed Laura a piece of paper.

"*Those chasing Death, tend to find her faster than they hoped*," Laura read aloud.

"Spooky," Torinn commented.

"I want to cast message to the others standing watch," Lerissa directed. "Guys, I think I found something, how are we doing?" she asked raising a hand to her ear.

"I don't know," Ront responded. "How are we doing?" he asked turning to Mr. R.

"Give me a perception check," Mr. R instructed.

Liam winced at his roll. "Well—it's a thirteen," he said through his teeth.

"You hear the normal few footsteps pass every so often," Mr. R explained. "Mostly guards doing their rounds, but every once in a while, a scholar of some sort runs by. Nothing seems to be amiss—" He trailed. He rolled a couple dice.

Ront raised his hand to his ear. "We're all clear—"

"Hey," Mr. R interrupted. "What's goin' on in the library?" His voice was scratchy and menacing. Like your typical cockney movie goon. "Why's the door open?"

"Scratch that," Ront continued. "We've got company!"

"What're we gonna do?" I whispered to him.

"Shhh!" Ront said raising his finger to his lips. *Don't let them hear us! Get against the wall and hide!* he signed.

"I cast a fog cloud as he approaches the door," Rolen whispered. "This will lower our chances of being seen." *If he passes through the door, take him out!* He finished in sign language.

"You guys watch as Rolen's eyes begin to glaze over and a fog begins to emerge from the floor beneath you," Mr. R described. "As the cloud grows thicker, your line of sight begins to shrink, and you lose sight of your companions. You hear the footsteps getting closer as the metal boots click against the stone floor."

"I ready my dagger," Ront said.

"And I, my axe," I added.

"Does it sound like he's inside the room now?" Rolen asked.

"The clicking sounds like it's passed through the door," Mr. R answered. "What's going on in here?" the guard hissed.

"I drop fog cloud and cast gust to clear the fog!" Rolen shouted "Now!"

"You all witness the fog begins to dissipate and then with a blast of air the cloud disappears. Roll initiative—"

"Twenty-three!" Liam blurted before his uncle could finish his sentence.

"Seventeen," I joined. We paused waiting for Ben to blurt out his roll. But he just sat there staring at his die.

"Rolen?" Mr. R asked. "What'd you get?"

"One," Ben sighed hanging his head in shame.

Liam and I both burst into laughter. Falling into each other. We laughed for a solid minute! We laughed until there were tears in our eyes and pain in our stomachs!

"You're kidding me?" Liam asked through his fit of laughter. "All that stealth work and you roll a one on our attack?'"

"Well instead of laughing, why don't you kill him?" Ben shouted.

"I'm gonna grab him from behind with my dagger at his throat and whisper in his scaly ear." Ront leaned in still giggling. "Make a sound and I gut you like the worthless pair of boots you are." He smiled manically.

"He ignores your warning and begins shouting at the top of his lungs," Mr. R responded. "Help! Intruders in the library! Intruders in the library—"

"I slit his throat," Ront interrupted. "Twenty-seven to hit."

He rolled damage before his uncle could respond. "Five damage."

"You drag your dagger across the leathery skin, cutting into his throat," Mr. R described. "He coughs with a gurgle as he collapses to the floor clutching his throat."

"I stop to listen for coming guards," Ront continued.

"They're coming, no missing that." Mr. R smiled.

"I start running," Rolen announced.

"I follow," I said.

"I'm going to drag the dying guard into the doorway and write 'RUN' on the floor with his blood," Ront directed.

He was getting a little scary with being a murderhobo lately. Anything he could kill, he killed—and quite gruesomely at that.

"As you bury your dagger in the skull of the dragonborn guard, you feel the rest of his body go limp under you as the life escapes him," Mr. R narrated.

"And then I book it back with the others," Ront said.

"What took you so long?" I asked.

"I had to leave them a message," he responded.

"Murderhobo?" I rolled my eyes.

"Murderhobo." he smiled.

"You guys begin to make your way down the spiraling staircase towards the library and your other companions, still hearing the closing guards clanging behind you," Mr. R described. "You finally reach your companions. Lerissa, Gimble, and Torinn. What do you do as you watch the other three in your party come barreling down towards you from their post upstairs?"

"Oh Lord," Lerissa said shaking her head. "Guess we'd better grab and go. I shove the book with the symbol in my pack."

"I grab a bunch of scrolls and books around the spot Lerissa took her book from and toss them in my bag of holding," Gimble said.

"Y—you can't do that!" Torinn stuttered in his old man voice. "Those are texts of learning in the Grand Library! If you take them, nobody will be able to learn from them!"

"Tor," Lerissa stopped him, putting her hand on his shoulder. "Who is going to be able to learn from these books and scrolls if they're locked away from the world? This library is more of a vault than a school."

"Ahh, I see," Torinn said scratching his chin. "I grab a bunch of books and scrolls and fill Gimble's bag as well!"

"Hey!" Gimble shouted at his brother. "This bag may have a bunch of space, but come on! We can't rescue the entire library!"

"Well," Torinn smiled. "We're gonna try!"

"At this point, all six of you are together," Mr. R said.

"What did you guys do?" Lerissa sighed.

"Well, we might have got ourselves caught," Ront responded.

"Of course you did," She groaned pinching the bridge of her nose between her thumb and finger. "Come on, everyone join hands."

"Why?" Torinn asked.

"Teleport out of—" She stopped. "We did that last time to get in, didn't we?" She rolled her eyes. "Crap."

"Now what?" I asked.

"We fight," Ront smiled.

"You're the rogue!" Lerissa shouted at him. "You're supposed to be able to sneak in and around things. Why do you keep wanting to fight?"

"Well, our only exit is most definitely blocked by this point," Ront reminded her.

"Actually," Torinn spoke up. "There is another way out. It's a secret doorway hidden in the library."

"Why didn't you tell us this before?" Rolen shouted.

"Nobody asked," Torinn shrugged. "Do we wanna use it?"

"Yes!" We all shouted together.

"Okay, okay," He said throwing his hands up. "Follow me—"

"Down there!" Mr. R interrupted, pointing. "Fire at will!"

"Crap!" Ront shouted.

"I need a dexterity check from all of you," Mr. R asked.

"Twelve," Torinn said.

"Fourteen," Gimble called out.

"Eighteen," Lerissa announced.

Followed by me, "Eighteen too!"

Ront cursed under his breath after looking at his roll. "Seven?" he winced. "I'm a freaking rogue and I can't dodge any ranged attacks?"

"All of you, except for Ront, manage to dive out of the way. Ront goes to make his leap out of the way and catches—" Mr. R rolled behind his screen. "Three bolts. One in the shoulder. One in your leg. And one in your stomach. Taking—six damage."

"Can I still make it to cover?" Ront asked.

"Yeah. You made the dive. You just happened to catch a few bolts on the way." Mr. R chuckled. "Let's roll initiative again."

"Seventeen," Gimble said.

"Twenty!" I cheered, throwing my fist into the air.

"Eighteen," Torinn announced.

"Ten," Rolen said.

"Nine," Ront sighed. "Can't I roll anything good?"

"Well, I got a four, so," Lerissa shrugged.

"Alright, Adrik. You're up first," Mr. R said pointing at me.

"I'm gonna whip out my javelin and give it a hurl at them," I smiled. "Sixteen hit?"

"Just makes it," Mr. R said.

I rolled my d6. "Seven damage."

"You come out and launch your javelin into one of the guards on the stairs. It hits him right in the shoulder and knocks him off the stairs. Causing him to plummet to his death."

"Nailed it!" I cheered. "I'm gonna try it again. Seventeen hits, dealing five damage." I calculated.

"This time you launch a javelin into another guard but he remains standing."

"Dang! Okay, that ends my turn then." I sighed.

"Torinn," Mr. R pointed at Daryl.

"I cast find path," Torinn responded. "This spell allows me to find the quickest and best route to any non-moving location I wish that is on the same plane as I am. I'm searching for my secret exit."

"As you cast this spell, whispering the incantation into your hands," Mr. R began. "A little ball of blue arcane light swirls into creation and floats out of your hands and onto the ground. It hovers in a circle at your feet before bobbing deeper into the library."

"Everyone, follow me!" Torinn shouted. "And I follow the spell."

"Alright. Gimble," Mr. R said turning to Jake.

"I wanna cast invisibility on myself and book it behind Tor," Gimble answered.

"You watch as Torinn chases after the ball of blue light he created. Gimble, in response to this, you play your tune of invisibility, disappearing from sight and running away into the aisle behind Torinn," Mr. R explained.

He clicked his keyboard and the image changed to a battle map on the screen. This map was a maze, with twists and turns, dead ends and even a couple drop-offs.

"The guards take their crossbows back over the railing and aim them back at you all—" He trailed for a second in thought. "But since you're all behind cover they can't manage a shot—so instead of shooting, they'll begin marching down the stairs again." He rolled a few dice behind his screen before writing in his notes. "Which moves to Rolen." He pointed the eraser of his pencil at Ben.

"I want to move out of cover and cast Stone Wall in front of us to give us more cover," Rolen explained.

"Okay. You all watch as Rolen jumps out from his cover to face the oncoming horde of guards clanking down the staircase. Moving his arms in a dramatic rising motion. A massive stone wall shoots out of the floor just feet in front of you guys, blocking the incoming attackers," Mr. R said, miming the arm motions.

"Go! Get out of here!" Rolen shouted. "I stay there holding the wall in place until everyone is safely away."

"Alright. That moves us to Ront," Mr. R said pointing at Liam.

"I want to grab these two," Ront pointed at Lerissa and me. "And start following where Torinn ran off to!"

"Okay. The next two actions are both of you," Mr. R said, also pointing at us.

"Well I'll go," Lerissa responded.

"I stay and fight alongside my brother," I said, clapping Ben on his back.

"You idiot!" Rolen yelled at me. "Go with them! I will be right behind you! Just go!"

"I'm not leaving you here alone!" I shouted back. "When that wall comes down, you're gonna need some help and I'm not leaving you here alone to get killed!"

"Fine!" Rolen stood up. "You wanna die with me? Once Lerissa and Ront get far enough out of danger, I'll drop the wall and burn both my wild shapes to shapeshift into a fire elemental!"

"With a completely emotionless expression, you watch as Rolen drops his hand that was holding up the wall, which now comes crashing down to the ground. And then with a smile creeping along his face, he bursts into flames. Before you, where once stood your half-elven friend now stands a humanoid fire elemental—still smiling at you," Mr. R said.

"Ha-ha!" I laughed. "Now we're talkin! I ready my axe."

"As you both ready for combat, the clanking guards finally make it up and over the pile of rubble and move in for their attacks!" Mr. R rolled a handful of dice from behind his screen, the dice all clicking together.

"I wanna use slam!" Rolen blurted.

"Alright, I'll give you an opportunity attack considering you prepared for the oncoming attack," Mr. R shrugged.

"Good!" Rolen smiled. "Twenty-four to hit."

"I'm gonna need eleven more of those hits," Mr. R chuckled after rolling more dice.

"Ugh," Rolen moaned. "One sec." He reached into his pocket and pulled his phone back out. Taking a few moments to open his phone and find the app he was looking for. "Eleven, fourteen, twenty-one, seven, fifteen, seven, twenty-three, eleven, seventeen, twelve, and twelve again," he said looking back up from his phone.

"Miss, miss, hit, miss, hit, miss, hit, miss, hit, miss, and miss," Mr. R listed with a chuckle.

"The ones I hit take five bludgeoning damage, and—" Rolen trailed off to calculate. "Three fire damage from burn."

"As you swing your arm at the advancing guards, some dodge the coming fist of fire, while some are not so lucky. Connecting with their snouts and cheeks, you burn a nice fist print into their faces." Mr. R described. "They are stunned by the punch coming so fast, but each one turns back at you and gives you an ominous smile as they wipe away the soot left from the punch. They seem unaffected by the burn." Mr. R mimicked the dragonborn wiping his chin. "You boys look like you're ready to die!" he snarled at us.

"As he says that," I interjected. "I rage, and bull rush them with my berserker axe!"

"Okay," Mr. R said. "Roll to attack."

"Sixteen," I said. I rolled for damage before he could ask. "Doing six damage. I want to attack this guard again with my second attack." I rolled my d20. "Twenty-seven to hit, doing—" I trailed off to roll damage. "Eight damage."

"As you hear the guard threaten you and your friends, you feel an overwhelming rush of anger flood your body. You let out a slight growl as you charge the guard in front of you." Mr. R began. "You under-swing your axe, burying it deep into the guard's stomach with a nasty and bloody splish sound; blood splattering all over. He goes limp on your axe. Instinctually you shake the body off and attack the next closest guard. Explain to me how this one dies." He asked me.

"Ooo," I grinned. "After I drop the dead body off my axe, I turn to the next guard, smile at him and say, Next. And I swing the axe over my head in a circular motion, chopping off his head!"

"With little resistance, you cut clean through the guard's neck. Sending his head flying across the aisle," Mr. R said circling his fingers around each other to show how the head flies.

"I wanna lick the blood off my lips and give a large smile at the next guy, frightening him!" I added.

"I need an intimidation roll," Mr. R said.

"But I can use an action to frighten a creature within thirty feet," I replied. And almost as fast as I could try to argue him I realized why he said that. "But I used both of my actions already," I sighed and rolled the dice. "Sixteen," I said.

"The guard looks a bit shaken by the pure brutality and gore he just witnessed," Mr. R explained. "But he tightens his grip and tries to attack you," he rolled behind his screen. "But he's too frightened to land the attack. Hitting your arm but doing no damage."

"As a reaction, I would love to end his life as well," I smiled. "Twenty-five to hit. Dealing seven damage."

"As he makes contact with his sword, you both have that awkward moment of eye contact. You watch as any form of confidence he had fades out of his eyes as you smile at him. And with a swift hack into his chest, you watch the life fade from his face and he falls limp and bloody to the floor."

"Anytime you wanna pick up some slack," I said to Rolen, laughing. "That'd be great!"

"Hey, I loosened those three for you. But you seem to be doing alright without me," Rolen chuckled.

"I need a wisdom saving throw from you, Adrik," Mr. R said.

"Crap," I muttered. I rolled my d20. "Well, that's not any better," I moaned. "Seven."

Mr. R smiled. "Since you were attacked and failed the wisdom saving throw, you go berserk. Attacking the next closest creature to you."

"I'm sorry," I said to Rolen. "Eighteen," I winced.

"Dude!" Rolen shouted. "Can I dodge?" He asked Mr. R.

"You'll have to roll for it and it will replace your AC defense." He responded.

"Well, they're the same number so I guess I'll chance it," Rolen sighed. He rolled his dice. "Oh boy!" He cheered. "Nat twenty, son!" He shouted, jumping out of his seat and slamming his hands against his hips.

"Rolen, as you watch your friend and ally suddenly become blood-thirsty as his eyes begin to bleed red into the iris. You realize that he's coming after you!" Mr. R narrated.

"When he swings at me, I wanna split in half to dodge his axe."

"As Adrik swings through your fiery midsection, your torso jumps off your lower half, separating in two, and reconnecting as the blade passes through you." Mr. R described.

"At this point. I would like to run!" Rolen announced.

"You turn and begin running down the aisle of books that your friends had gone down before. Behind you charges Adrik in a frenzied rage. And behind him, a trail of fire cascading up along the bookshelves," Mr. R said. "You can hear shouting and screams as the guards behind you try to put out the flames."

"Crap!" Rolen shouted. "I drop my elemental form and continue running from Adrik," he said.

"You both continue running at top speeds until you suddenly fly through a hole in the wall in front of you. Both falling—and falling—and falling." Mr. R clicked his keyboard and the image in the table changed to a cliffside image on the side of what I assume is the library's outer walls. "And then *splash*! You both crash into the water below! Adrik, your berserk and rage effects wear off. Take down one point of exhaustion."

"Well," I sighed. "We're in trouble Rolen. Dwarfs don't swim."

THREE
THE ADVENTURE HEADS SOUTH

"Rolen, as you begin to become aware of where you are and start swimming through the aggressive currents, you notice Adrik splashing around in a feeble attempt to stay above the surface, gasping for the few breaths of air he can get before getting swept under by the current," Mr. R described.

"Crap, crap, crap!" Rolen cursed. "Ummm, I'll cast control water and redirect the flow so that I can move to scoop him up and move towards the cliff wall under the library."

"Okay." Mr. R cleared his throat. "As you begin to empty your mind of panic, you focus the arcane energy flowing through you as the current of the thrashing water begins to move you towards Adrik. Who, as of now, has lost his battle against the water and is sinking."

"I want to direct the water flow up towards me then, so he stops sinking," Rolen said. "And then snag him and go towards the wall."

"The water begins to flow up like a fountain. Foaming as the water crashes back into itself. But Adrik keeps on sinking," Mr. R said.

"Oh come on!" Rolen groaned. "Then I polymorph myself

into—a—ummm..." He stuttered as he began searching through manuals looking for something to change into. "Um—a giant octopus!"

"In all the commotion and watching your friend sink deeper into the dark waters, you begin to transform into a giant octopus," Mr. R began. "Watching your arms and legs as they begin to grow suction cups and turn a reddish-orange color splitting into two different tentacles. You begin to swim down into the water, chasing after your sinking companion. Deeper and deeper into the dark abyss. You finally are able to reach him, but as you try to swim up with him, you feel yourself being dragged deeper down with him. You realize that Adrik is way too heavy."

"If you weren't so fat," Rolen sighed. He clicked his tongue trying to figure out what to do.

Mr. R rolled some dice behind his screen before speaking up. "Adrik, you take two suffocation damage."

"Crap!" Rolen cursed. "I'm gonna drop my polymorph. And then recast polymorph on Adrik. Turning him into a mouse."

"As you both sink deeper into the water, you drop your octopus form. Trying to turn Adrik into a mouse." Mr. R paused. "Is Adrik willing?"

"At this point, he's willing to do anything to stay alive!" I responded.

"Then you feel yourself begin to morph and change. Your body shrinking to a miniature size. It's a weird sensation feeling your entire anatomy change. Then you feel a massive hand grab you."

"I start swimming up as fast as I can," Rolen said.

"What feels like forever eventually comes to an end as you surface from the water and begin swimming towards the cove under the cliff wall."

"Once we get out of the water, I drop his polymorph," Rolen said.

"And as you both lay there panting for air on the beach in a little cove in the wall, the rest of your party comes walking down a stone path that leads all the way up to the hole in the wall you came through." Mr. R smiled.

"Are you two done almost dying?" Lerissa asked sarcastically. "Because we need to get going before those guards end up catching us."

"As you say that, you all begin to smell something burning," Mr. R said.

Lerissa buried her face into her hands. "I'm guessing that was the two of you?" she asked, her words muffled in her hands.

"You turn to take a look at the hole in the wall that you all escaped from—and there is a plume of smoke pouring out of the hole," Mr. R responded.

"What the hell did you do?" Lerissa sighed.

"What? We had to fight off the guards." I shrugged. "I don't know what your problem is. So what part of the library caught fire—"

"Part of the library is on fire?" Torinn shouted. "I turn to look at the plume of smoke."

"How did the two of you manage to set the library on fire?" Gimble laughed.

"It wasn't on purpose," Rolen defended.

"Oh great, it was just an accident!" Torinn laughed hysterically. "He accidentally destroyed the greatest collection of knowledge known to the material plane! Just—an accident." Torinn began to grow increasingly scary as he laughed more and more. "Just an accident he said! He didn't mean it! Good god, what is Pelor going to say about this?" he mumbled to himself as he dropped his face into his hands.

"Way to go, you two," Ront said slapping me on the back. "You two successfully destroyed one of the last remaining archives that dates back beyond the fall of Oculous." He clapped slowly leaning back into his chair. "Brava! Brava! Bravissima!" He laughed. "Man, what would Ioun say?"

"Shut up!" Rolen snapped. "You can't say squat! The only reason you believe in the gods is because you died and they felt pity for you so they brought you back."

"Let us not forget, it was my death and sacrifice that saved your sister." Ront folded his arms and smirked. It was the infamous grin Liam had that set off Ben.

You could see the rage in his eyes swell. "Are you serious!" Rolen shouted. "You're just gonna bring that up again? How many weeks will this go on?"

"As many as it takes to remind you what we're doing here!" Ront shouted back. "And I pull out the Raven Dagger."

"Oh now, what? You're gonna kill me?" Rolen snapped. "Send my soul to the abyss like all these other pathetic souls you've taken for her?" His knuckles grew bone white as he clenched his pencil, the faintest sound of wood splitting coming from the pencil. "I want to do fiery fists!" He said through his teeth.

"Ooo big man with the magic fists," Ront mocked. "What're you gonna do? I know you won't hit me. You don't have the guts—"

"I want to do fiery-stone fists and punch Ront," Rolen snarled. "Natural twenty," he said staring down Liam.

"Reaction to throw the dagger behind him?" Ront asked his uncle.

"I'll give it to you," Mr. R nodded. "You all watch as Rolen's fiery fists bulk up as his skin becomes a fiery fist of stone. He winds up to punch Ront. And as he releases the punch, Ront throws the Raven Dagger into the sand behind Rolen. And within milliseconds you watch as Rolen is teleported..." Mr. R trailed and pointed at Liam.

"I teleport him upside down, over the water, about thirty feet in the air," Ront said. "Give him a moment to cool down."

"And all of the sudden you hear Rolen hit the water with a big sploosh," Mr. R said miming the splashing water with his hands.

"I just swim back to the beach," Rolen sighed rolling his eyes.

"Are we all done with acting like children?" Lerissa asked.

"You know us," Gimble laughed. "And I wanna begin playing my violin softly."

Mr. R clicked his keyboard and the sounds of crashing waves and a soft violin began to play. "So what do you guys do?"

"Well, I need a rest before I can teleport us anywhere," Lerissa said.

"Then let me play the tune for my mansion," Gimble responded.

"You all listen as the tune changes for a moment. And there in the cliff wall, an arcane door appears," Mr. R described.

"Let's all go to the lobby. Let's all go to the lobby," Gimble sang and he mimed walking.

"I follow," I said.

"Me too," Lerissa joined.

"I'm gonna wait for nature boy here to get back to the shore," Ront sighed.

"I walk right past him and go inside," Rolen growled.

"Aw come on Rolen," Ront moaned. "We're still friends, aren't we?"

"I just go inside, no response," Rolen said.

"Well, I guess I'll go inside—"

"It was just an accident they said," Torinn interrupted mumbling to himself. "They didn't mean to destroy the library."

"Never mind. I'll go scoop up Mr. Lost-his-mind and take him inside," Ront said.

"They destroyed it, Ront," Torinn mumbled. "Everything is gone. You know the only other library that large is lost? No one can find it."

"I know buddy," Ront consoled him. "I know. But there's nothing we can do about it now. We just need to pray and hope that there are magic users here who can restore the lost books."

"You saw how large that library was," Torinn snapped. "Do you know how many magic users that will take?"

"That's why we pray they can restore it," Ront said again. "Now come on, let's get inside before the guards find us. And I help lead him into the mansion in the wall."

"Alright. When you all come into the mansion, you're greeted by an arcane servant like always. Some with food. Some with towels. Some offering to help carry anything."

"I head to my room and meditate," Rolen said.

"I think I will do the same before I rest for the night," Lerissa said.

"I want to escort crazy-pants here to his room and make sure he's alright," Ront started.

"An accident, Ront. It was all just... an accident," Torinn stammered.

"And then I'm gonna go to Rolen's room and try to talk to him," Ront said.

"I think it's due time for a good drink," I said trying to break the tension in the air. "Join me, Gimble?"

"I think you're right." Gimble nodded to me with a laugh. "I lead the way down into the cellar."

"And I happily follow." I chuckled.

"Alright," Mr. R said clapping his hands together. "Adrik and Gimble, is there anything special you wanna do before I go to these two again?"

"Yeah," Gimble said. "Before we start, I pull a servant aside and ask them to just make sure that Rolen and Ront don't kill each other."

"The servant nods and heads down the corridor," Mr. R said.

"And then I take Adrik into my vast alcohol cellar. Swinging the massive wooden doors open," Gimble explained. "Revealing my expansive collection of ales, wines, meads, and spirits. The seemingly endless hall of kegs and bottles. With a nice little table set up in the entrance area with food on it."

"I promptly take a seat and ask the servant for a large flagon of ale," I said with a bellowing laugh. "And I start chowing down on the biggest piece of meat at the table," I continued, before taking a large piece of sausage off my plate and popping it in my mouth.

"Alright." Mr. R nodded. "Ront. Rolen. How does this go down?"

"I'm gonna knock on his door," Ront said.

"I don't respond," Rolen said with his eyes closed.

"I knock again," Ront said, knocking on the table. "Come on, let me in."

Ben just kept his eyes closed. "I'm gonna keep on meditating." He drew in a large breath and slowly let it out.

"I just keep on knocking," Ront said.

"I cast druidcraft, creating a skunk odor under the door," Rolen said calmly.

"You start to get a sense of a familiar smell," Mr. R said raising his eyebrow a little. "This smell that causes you to scrunch your face. The nasty aroma swelling in your nose."

"Come on, Rolen," Ront moaned through fake coughs. "Can't we just talk?"

"I just keep on meditating," Rolen said.

"Ugh." Ront groaned. "I didn't want to do this. I stab the Raven Dagger into the door and teleport myself into the room."

"I continue meditating," Rolen sighed.

"Are you really gonna stay mad at me?" Ront moaned. "You did destroy an ancient library. And honestly, even if I wasn't a pawn to the Raven Queen, that Ioun comment was funny. Come on, the god of knowledge? You destroyed a library? It was funny!" He awkwardly shrugged.

Rolen raised his chin to the sky.

"Does this have to do with something else outside the table?" Liam bowed his head. "Look, I'm sorry. I didn't mean for you to take the fall for it. And I definitely didn't want to ditch you. I was a being a bad friend. If I could go back I would!"

Ben let out a heavy sigh. "I destroyed it trying to save all of you," he said calmly.

Liam blinked for a moment, looking confused at Ben. Then his eyes lit up with understanding. "But like, how was setting the place on fire saving us?"

"There was a whole army of guards coming after us. What else was I supposed to do? Let them catch us?" Rolen asked. His voice getting a little louder.

"You don't think we could have helped fend them off?" Ront asked.

"No!" Rolen shouted. "It's not that I didn't think you could stand up for yourself. None of that was the reason. I was giving an escape!"

"Well, then what was the reason?" Ront asked, shifting in his chair.

"You're kidding me right?" Rolen asked hysterically. "What's the reason I gave you all an escape? You can't be this dense, Liam!"

"I feel like we've strayed away from this being in the game," Mr. R said.

"I'm sorry," Ben sighed. "That was my bad." He drew a deep breath and slowly let it out. "I gave you all an escape to make sure you all could safely make it out with the books. I didn't mean to set the library on fire. I got too deep in the moment of battle and it went awry." Rolen closed his eyes once again, returning his character to his meditation.

"That's all I wanted to know," Ront said with a smile. "And I walk out of the room." He shifted to face Ben. "I stop in the doorway before leaving. By the way, thank you."

"Alrighty," Mr. R nodded. "You all begin to wind down for the night. Finding your own ways towards sleep. Some from pure exhaustion. Some from a heavy amount of drinking. But you all manage to get some rest. Except for Rolen... you have a more eventful evening."

"Oh lord," Rolen sighed.

"During your meditation, you begin to get visions. Some vague, some vivid. After Ront leaves your room, you began to feel a falling sensation. Falling into the black void." He clicked his keyboard and the tv went black. And then it began to swirl with purples and reds. Until the colors began to mix into a bloody crimson red. "Suddenly you hit what feels like ground... but it's still a black void. And then you get a sharp pain that shoots into your head. Like a spear through your brain. And a voice begins to speak to you..." He cleared his throat and took a drink from his soda. "Forget us. Stop searching for Death's Hand." He growled.

His voice going in and out of different tones and scratchiness. Sometimes sounding close and whispered. Other times far and loud. It was very eerie. "Stop looking for the Elven wizard girl. Forget about Reita. Drop your arms and go home. Or suffer —" he clicked his keyboard. "The consequences!" And the screen erupted into flames. "Suddenly you see a gigantic hand reach out over you. Hanging from the fingers on strings are each of your companions' limp bodies. And then a face moves in from the darkness."

He clicked his keyboard again and this image of a squid-like face appears from the flames. It's a Mind Flayer!

"A face with tentacles peers from the darkness, towering over you. You feel the pain in your skull increase. You begin to hear screams. The wailing of your companions begging you for help. Begging for you to end their suffering. Begging you to kill them..." Mr. R said. "You feel overwhelmed with the cries of pain and anguish. The pain in your skull begins to spread across your head—more like a hand now rather than a spear—as you begin to rise off the ground you laid upon, and you move towards the flailing tentacles on the Illithid's face. As they move aside exposing its mouth with a forked tongue and sharp teeth in the front. You're dropped into the massive mouth. With a rushing sensation... you find yourself back in your room in the mansion. In the same spot, you last remembered, sitting in a cold, freezing sweat."

"W—what was th—that?" Rolen muttered under his breath. "I wanna cast produce flame and sit and warm myself up. Just staring into the flames."

"Okay." Mr. R cleared his throat again. "You all stir and wake at your own time. Your armor and weapons are freshly cleaned, polished, and sharpened. A grand breakfast is waiting in the dining room, and servants are waiting outside each of your rooms to help you with anything."

"I walk out of my room with no pants on and a mug," I said with a smile. "I hand the mug to the servant and say; Fill 'er up and meet me at the dining table."

"They take the mug from you and walk down the hall towards the cellar," Mr. R described.

"I want to study the book we discovered in the library," Lerissa said.

"Give me an investigation check," Mr. R asked.

"Twenty-four," Lerissa said.

"Alright," Mr. R said sitting up. "As you flip through the tome in your hands you read stories and accounts of the horrible things Death's Hand has done to the world. There are sections on the genocides and slaughters of what the book refers to as 'inferior beings.' This extensive list includes gnomes, halflings, all half beings, orcs, ogres. Pretty much anything that isn't pure-bred Elf and Human."

"This is barbaric," Lerissa whispered. "Is there anything in here about the killing of Rolen's tribe?"

"There is a section in there about how one of their more radical followers had slaughtered a tribe of druids. And how it disgraced the member from the order," Mr. R answered.

"So Reita wasn't actually Death's Hand?" Lerissa asked.

"From what you continue to read, you begin to clue in that Reita broke away from the cult to begin her own chapter of Death's Hand. But there isn't much more than that. Nothing about her influence or her followers. It just seems to stop talking about the 'disgraced'."

"So Reita acted on her own?" Lerissa whispered to herself. "So what does Death's Hand still want with me?"

"As you reach the end of the tome, you notice the blank pages in the back... are being filled with words," Mr. R said. He clicked his keyboard and the screen turned a brownish parchment color. Then writing began to appear.

Located young wizard girl and will bring her to the ruins of the Southlands for the ritual of revivification

"What the hell?" Lerissa mumbled. "They've got Elfi!" she shouted. "I run to find Rolen!"

"You find him still in his room," Mr. R said.

"I pound on the door! Rolen! Rolen!" She shouted smashing her fist into the table. "I found her! I think I found Elfi!"

"I open the door—pale-faced and still sweaty," Rolen described.

"W—what's wrong with you?" Lerissa asked. "You don't look so good."

"I—I had a rough night... nightmares and stuff," Rolen lied. "Like the ones I used to have after Reita killed our family."

"Okay..." she said skeptically. "But they never made you look like you've been doing drugs and not sleeping for a couple days. Something's wrong here," she said eyeing her brother.

"I'm fine, Riss," He said, waving her off. "I—I just didn't rest well. Let me get something to wake me up and I'll be fine." Ben mumbled just before he slammed his head against the table. "And Rolen passes out in the doorway," he said with his face in the table.

"I drop down to scoop him up and I cast—" She trailed off looking through her spells. "Crap! I don't have anything to help you. Ummm." She hummed. "I call for one of the servants and say; I need some water and Torinn. Now!" She shouted.

"Within seconds a servant comes running back with water. While Torinn, you are interrupted by a servant trying to get you to come with them," Mr. R described.

"Huh? Oh yes, that's right, you don't speak," Torinn said squinting over his glasses at Mr. R. "I presume you want me to follow you?"

Mr. R nodded in response. "And then the servant begins to walk with some urgency down the hallway."

"I take the hint and follow him," Torinn said.

"As you round the corner, you see Lerissa on the floor holding a pale Rolen, his eyes glossed over," Mr. R said.

"Oh good lord Pelor, what happened to him?" Torinn asked, pretending to be shocked.

"Don't just stand there and stare at us. Come fix him!" Lerissa shouted at Torinn.

"Right!" He snapped to attention. "I kneel down beside them both and I cast lesser restoration on him." Daryl reached over to Ben and placed his hand on his shoulder... and then smacked him on the back side of his head.

"Ow!" Ben yelled. "What the hell was that?"

"I was casting the spell to wake you up." Torinn smiled. "But you're restored from anything affecting you. You should be fine now."

"You all watch as Torinn's amulet begins to glow on his chest. He reaches down to touch Rolen and his face gains some color back and his eyes flutter back open," Mr. R described.

"Rolen?" Lerissa asked. "Are you okay? Can you hear me?"

"W—what?" Rolen stammered. "Y—yeah, yeah I'm fine. What happened?"

"You passed out in the doorway on me," Lerissa explained to him. "What happened? You told me you had the nightmares again. Is that what happened?"

"No. No, no, no. Not the nightmares again." Rolen shook his head. "Those are long over. A demon I've managed to bury. This wasn't like anything I've had before," Rolen said, rubbing his head. "This was much more than a dream. It was a message."

"What do you mean, 'a message'?" Torinn chimed in. His eyebrow raised with skepticism.

"I mean some magic being sent me a message," Ben tried to explain. "Threatening our lives. Telling me to give up my mission—" Rolen trailed off. "Or they'd— He'd— I'd be killed."

"Who threatened you?" Lerissa asked.

"I—" Rolen stopped and contemplated. "I don't... I don't know." He sighed. "I didn't see a face."

"Well, why would someone want you to stop tracking a death cult?" Lerissa asked, eyeing her brother. "Matt," she turned towards Mr. R. "Can I insight him to see if he's hiding anything?"

"I don't see why not," Mr. R said. "I need a deception check out of Rolen though."

"You first," Lerissa said to Rolen. "I wanna see how well you lie."

Rolen rolled his dice and then looked back at his sister with a smile. "Nat... twenty!"

Lerissa rolled her die. She looked to the ceiling and closed her eyes as she dropped the die on the table. She then proceeded to sit slumped in her chair. "Sixteen." She glared at Rolen.

"He seems to be telling you everything he knows," Mr. R chuckled.

"I swear I don't know what to make of this," Rolen pleaded with Lerissa. "But I feel like we should heed the warning. What if this really is too much for us? We already lost a party-member once to this mission. And I don't think that we will get lucky a second time with the gods."

"Are you serious?" Torinn interrupted. "We were given this mission by the gods! And you're gonna throw it away because some magic-user told you to?"

"I'm sorry," Rolen snapped. "I don't know about you, but I'm sick of losing people. My tribe, my friends, my sleep!"

"But you're gonna let them slaughter innocents? Because you had a nightmare?" Torinn shouted back.

"What the hell is with everyone belittling my opinions for?" Rolen asked. "All I want is for you all to be safe. For goodness sakes, I'm a damn druid! I'm supposed to protect nature and all living beings. Why can I not be concerned for our safety?" he shouted now addressing the whole group.

"Rolen, settle down," Torinn said calmly. "You are getting worked up over nothing. You need to put in perspective what we're doing. We risk and sacrifice our lives for the greater good. I get that you're worried about us being killed. As the group cleric and healer, I share that concern. But you need to see what our sacrifice is for." He took a sip of water. "I want to open my amulet and show him the major image spell inside it."

"You watch as Torinn reaches for his amulet and pulls it out so you can see it in full detail, the white and gold sun emblem engraved on it glinting in the light. He runs his finger over it and the sun begins to twist, and you hear the locking mechanism click." Mr. R clicked his tongue. "And the amulet opens and reveals a swirling arcane pool inside. Torinn dips his finger in it and it disturbs the flow. The water substance begins to rise like flames and taking on humanoid figures. Like a jewelry box, the figures begin to move and perform actions. What does the amulet show them?"

"The amulet shows the attack on Dracomear; when the dragon attacked. That child there," He pointed to his palm. "She is standing over her parent's corpses. She's in shock and doesn't know how to process the situation at hand." Torinn explained. "And this is what I want you to see..."

He reached into his phone and slid the screen open. He tapped around for a second and then a moment later turned the phone to us. There was a painting of a dragonborn in armor almost identical to Torinn's description. The dragonborn was fighting back a blast of fire and shielding this little girl from the blast. From his arms, a transparent shield separated the dragonborn from his demise. He swiped to the next picture and it was of the same scene only this time another dragonborn appeared carrying the little girl. This dragonborn was identical to the other in the image.

"This is the fall of Nadarr Yarjerit..." He paused. "My brother. This is the sacrifice he made so that one day I could do the same to save another! That is the sacrifice we make every time we set foot outside; to protect those who can't protect themselves." Torinn said, turning off his phone. "But as long as we're together, no one has to make that sacrifice alone."

Rolen drew in a deep breath. "You're right." He ran his hand across his face. I can't tell if he's thinking or just trying to collect himself before blasting Torinn. But whatever was in his head, he never said any more.

"So is there more?" Lerissa asked.

"N—no," Rolen lied.

"Well then come on and get some breakfast." She sighed. "I have some information for everyone about your girlfriend."

"You found Elfi?" Rolen perked up. "I mean... she's not my girlfriend." He sat back, trying to play off his excitement.

FOUR

ESCAPE FROM DRACOMEAR

"You all make your way to the dining room in some form or fashion," Mr. R said. "On the table is a massive assortment of fruits, eggs, meats, and juices all set out and ready to be eaten."

"Can I assume that I've been here for a while eating and drinking?" I asked.

"And you all see Adrik with his face buried in a plate of breakfast. Little bits of egg and meat in his beard and a cask of ale sitting next to him," Mr. R explained.

"Nobody cares about that," Lerissa interrupted. "I clear a spot and drop the book on the table. I open it to the page with the writing on it."

"You all watch Lerissa slam the book on the table with a thud!" Mr. R describes, slamming his fist onto the table. "And on the pages are the writing from before." He motioned to the screen that still had the writing on it.

"It sounds like they found Elfi and are taking her to the Southland Ruins," Lerissa explained.

"Are you sure about that?" Ront asked.

"What do you mean am I sure?" Lerissa shot back. "Who else could it be? Does it look like they have me?"

"No." Ront shrugged. "But read it again. It just says located. Not actually taken," he said pointing to the words on the screen.

"Well, it still can't be me," Lerissa defended. "We're in a magic mansion inside the wall of a cliff! There's no way they found me! How could they even know where we're at?"

"Well..." Rolen chimed in. "I did set an ancient library on fire. And if the Dracomearians are as smart as they're said to be, we've been revealed to Death's Hand. Especially if they notice a certain book is missing from their inventory."

"But there's no way that they could have done that," Torinn joined in. "Even with all their strongest arcane beings, there's no way they could restore the entire library that quick!"

"Yes that's true," Ront contemplated. "But they knew where we were at in the library before we ran, so maybe they restored that section first," He explained.

"It can't be me, though," Lerissa pleaded. "Reita wanted me, not them. She isn't a part of Death's Hand."

"What do you mean?" Rolen asked.

"This book is an archive of Death's Hand," Lerissa said. "I flip through the book looking for the section on Reita and her exile."

"You all watch Lerissa flip through this book for a couple seconds before she slams her finger onto a line of text a couple pages back," Mr. R described. "It talks about a tiefling woman who pleaded to the master about a child. She told the higher powers of Death's Hand that this child possesses the power necessary to destroy and recreate life; that this child could build the army of undead that they dreamed of. But the council denied her request to slaughter her own people for one child." He paused to take a drink. "So she went out on her own. She slaughtered an entire camp of tiefling refugees looking for this child. Killing thousands of her own kind. When the fires died and the blood stopped flowing across the ground—the child was nowhere to be found. The woman tracked the child for months, killing innocent people left and right. She destroyed whole villages and towns looking for the child. The council warned her that if she continued this tirade for a child, they would exile her and destroy her attunement to the arcane energy of the plane. But she persisted."

"Wait," Rolen interrupted. "If she was exiled and they removed her arcane powers, how did she do all that magic when we battled her last time? Like raising the dead orc to come after us?" he asked.

"Hang on," Lerissa said. "Maybe they didn't take her powers. Keep reading."

"The book continues telling about the woman and her vendetta. The months of tracking that lead her to the tribe of druids who fostered the child she longed to take. The western nomads of Myciya. She destroyed them, but still did not have the child," Mr. R recited. "She returned to the council empty-handed. The master was furious with her negligence and disregard for the council's orders. They sentenced her to be removed from the order and have her arcane abilities torn from her through tortuous means, but before they could detain her she destroyed the chamber and vanished."

"See, what did I say?" Lerissa gloated. "They didn't want me. They were gonna kill one of their strongest because that's how little they wanted me. There's no way it's me they found for this ritual."

Ront pursed his lips. "I guess not." He scratched his chin in thought for a moment. "Then I guess let's eat and get moving. We have a wizard to save."

"Oh, way ahead of you guys!" I said through a mouth full

of pizza.

"So you all sit down and eat. Fueling for the journey ahead. You refill your water sacks and flasks and collect your equipment from your rooms, meeting back in the front entrance," Mr. R narrated.

"To the Southlands?" Lerissa asked.

"To the Southlands!" I cheered.

"To the Southlands," Ront mumbled.

"You all walk out the massive ethereal doors, leading you out to the cold out cove where you all remember standing the previous afternoon," Mr. R said. "The icy ocean spray chills your skin to the touch as it blasts you in the face. Looking up, the gray skies hide any chance of the sun delivering warmth."

"Well, how do we propose getting to the Southlands?" Ront asked.

"Teleport there," Lerissa responded. "How else?"

"How would you like to use the teleport spell?" Mr. R asked.

"I want to cast from memory and send us off target so we don't end up in the middle of a death cult ceremony," Lerissa answered. "Everyone grab hands. I focus my thoughts on the Southland Ruins. To the spot Rolen and I used to camp when we were younger," she explained.

"Does everyone grab hands?" Mr. R asked. We all nodded in response. "Alright then, you all link hands with one another and begin to feel the arcane energy flow through you. As you're all pulled off your feet with a bright flash of white light, you all feel the familiar rushing feeling of teleportation. And then... nothing. It takes you all a moment to gather your senses and for your eyes to adjust. And once your fogginess clears, you notice that you are not in the ruins. In fact, you recognize this spot you're in. This is the area you camped in before sneaking into Dracomear."

"What happened?" Torinn asked. "This isn't the Southlands. This is just outside Dracomear! We camped here!"

"You all watch as Torinn points out the place where your fire had once burned, the charcoaled wood still sitting in the middle of a stone circle," Mr. R described.

"W—what?" Lerissa stuttered looking down at her hands. "I swear I was going to the ruins."

"That, my dear, might be true," Mr. R smiled. His voice calm, yet intimidating. "And from behind the trees, a dark human man walks into the clearing. His face is partially obscured by a black hood. Following behind him are what seems like dozens of armored soldiers. Each one in the same black studded leather armor and a faceless mask. Some are carrying bows, while others carry axes and swords."

"Who's there?" I growled. "And I pull out my axe and ready it."

"Don't you recognize us?" The man chuckled maniacally. "And you watch as he turns his forearm up and rolls his sleeve back. And there, scarred into his arm, is the raven insignia you all recognize as Death's Hand," Mr. R said, rolling up his sleeve.

"I pull out my raven dagger and my venom dagger," Ront announced. "How did you find us?" he snarled.

"My dear boy," the man shook his head and chuckled a little more. "You really think that we don't have members hidden everywhere? Don't you think that maybe one of our followers might have spotted you in Dracomear? That someone might have known we wanted you and contacted us in hopes of compensation?"

"So someone ratted us out?" Ront interrogated.

"Not just anyone..." Mr. R's grin grew into an ominous smile. "And you all watch as the man motions to two of his soldiers from behind him. They're dragging a humanoid being into the clearing, a bag covering their head. The two soldiers drop the bound humanoid before you all and remove the bag. And there, bound on the ground, a young gold and copperish dragonborn man looks up at you all. His face is bloody and beaten, and one of his eyes so swollen that he can't even open it. And there around his neck, an amulet identical to that of Torinn's."

"Kriv!" Torinn shouted. "I collapse in front of him and hold on to him," he explained. "My boy. What have you done to my boy?" he sobbed.

"I don't know what you're talking about..." The man said. "The cloaked man kneels down next to Kriv and pulls his own hood off. Revealing his entire face. The left side of his complexion is scarred with what appears to be both fire and acid burns," Mr. R described.

"What did you do to him?" I shouted.

"I did nothing," The man straightened his posture. "I was simply the messenger. I was sent to find you six by whatever means I deemed appropriate. I simply asked young Kriv here some easy questions. What's your name, how's your father, how's Pelor—" He stopped and that smile curled back across his face again. "Where's your father?"

"So you attacked him?" Lerissa shouted. "And I move at him."

"As you try to move, three soldiers step forward aiming their weapons at you," Mr. R explained.

"I would like to go invisible," Gimble chimed in.

"Okay. Where are you standing at this point?" Mr. R asked.

"I was standing behind Ront," Gimble explained. "I want to hide myself from these creeps. And then I want to climb up Ront's back onto his shoulder while telling him." He leaned forward to whisper across the table. "Don't say anything, it's me. I'm invisible. Just act normal."

"I just casually nod," Ront responded.

"So if you really just asked questions, why is he nearly dead?" Lerissa asked. "You keep talking like nothing has happened here, but Kriv's face says otherwise."

"Oh no, I only asked questions," the man repeated. "My associates here might have had a little fun with him after he decided we were no longer having a friendly chat," the man said, running his fingers across the scars on the left side of his face.

"You monsters!" Torinn growled. "And I want to blast him with my fire breath!"

"Eleven on his dex save," Mr. R announced.

Torinn gritted his teeth as he rolled. "Eleven fire damage."

"You all watch Torinn take a step towards the man, and then a blast of flames erupts from his mouth. It engulfs the man and you hear his screams. When the flames clear, you see the already burnt half of the man's face is now black and crispy," Mr. R described. "I need everyone to roll initiative."

"Seventeen," Torinn growled through his still gritted teeth.

"Eight," I winced.

"Twenty," Gimble laughed.

"Eleven," Ront said.

"Nineteen," Rolen jumped.

"Seven," Lerissa announced.

"Alright, Gimble. You're first," Mr. R said.

"Well there goes my stealth," Gimble joked. "I'm gonna cast dominate person on one of his archers. Wisdom saving throw."

"Ten," Mr. R said.

"Listen closely. Not for very much longer..." Gimble sang. "I've got to, keep control."

"As Gimble becomes visible again, perched on Ront's shoulder, you hear him singing this tune. But nothing seems different at the moment," Mr. R explained. "It's your turn still."

"Then let me tell my new friend to attack Two-Face over there," Gimble laughed. "Ugly up the rest of his face."

"And out of nowhere, one of the soldiers looses an arrow at the man." Mr. R rolled his dice. "And it drills into his shoulder."

"That's right son!" Gimble cheered.

"Traitor! Kill them all!" The man snarled. "Rolen, you're up."

"I'm gonna cast flaming sphere," Rolen said. "Centralized on Mr. Dent there."

Gimble reached over and fist bumped Rolen.

"Well, he failed his dexterity save," Mr. R said.

"Then burn!" Rolen threatened as he rolled his dice. "Eleven fire damage."

"Seems like a common occurrence with fire damage tonight," Mr. R chuckled. "Suddenly a ball of fire amasses out of nowhere, incinerating some soldiers and burning the man even more," he described. "Kill... them!" the man struggled.

"Torinn," Mr. R pointed at Daryl.

"I get up off my knees and walk over to this creep," Torinn narrated. "I cast spiritual weapon in the shape of a spear floating behind him. And I walk him back into it."

"You all see an arcane spear come into existence behind the man," Mr. R began. "As Torinn walks towards him, he backs away out of fear. Kill him! Kill him now! He shouts at his soldiers. He hobbles backward until..." He motioned to Torinn.

"Until he bumps into the tip of the spear." Torinn scowled. "And then I pull my hand towards me and bring the spear forward through his midsection."

"Ack!" Mr. R pretended to choke. He began laughing in defeat. "You're no better than me now, are you?"

"I will never be close to anything like you." Torinn snarled.

"And with twelve piercing damage, I pull the spear all the way through him."

"As the spear pulls itself through his abdomen, he goes limp and collapses to the floor," Mr. R described. "Ront, your turn."

"I pull my short bow and prep it for whatever idiot decides to attack next," Ront explained.

"Adrik," Mr. R pointed to me.

"I hold my axe still ready for whoever makes the next move," I said. "Now, who wants to get crazy?"

"Lerissa?" Mr. R turned to Laura.

"I throw a fire bolt at the tree behind the soldiers," she said. "Go back to your sewers and tell your people we do not fear you! Tell your council that we are coming for them! And tell your master—his time has come!"

"Make me an intimidation roll," Mr. R asked.

"Seventeen," Lerissa responded.

"You watch the soldiers exchange looks of fear before turning back into the trees," Mr. R narrated.

"Yeah, that's right!" I laughed. "Go home and cry, ya little babies!"

"Well," Lerissa sighed. "I guess you were right Ront. It was me."

"It doesn't matter who was right or wrong now," Ront responded. "They know where and how to find us. Which means that nowhere is safe anymore. And no one is safe."

"Kriv," Torinn broke in. "Kriv, are you okay? Can you hear me, son?"

"I—I'm sorry," Kriv replied. "They wouldn't stop. No matter how much I fought back. They just kept going. Even after I told them that I knew where you were. They just kept torturing me."

"I'm so sorry, Kriv." Torinn wiped a tear from his cheek. "I never wanted this to come to what it has. I never wanted anyone to get hurt because of me." His eyes began to fill with tears. "And I cast cure wounds on him."

"I didn't want to tell them," Kriv whimpered. "But they just kept casting spells and beating me. At one point I'm pretty sure I died. They killed me!" he said hysterically. "I saw them! I saw Nadarr and Pelor! They were trying to save me."

"They won't hurt you any longer, Kriv," Torinn said. "Never again."

"You feel as the spell begins to take effect, his ribs forming back into one piece. The swelling in his face begins to go down. The healing is taking effect," Mr. R described.

"You saw her?" Torinn asked. "You saw Pelor?"

"Yeah," Kriv nodded. "But what do you mean 'her'? Pelor... is a man."

Ront perked up. "I'm sorry. Did I just hear you say that Pelor is a man?"

"Yeah," Kriv nodded again. "I saw him with my uncle. They were trying to pull me out of my body and into the afterlife."

"But I've met Pelor. She was there when I died. She brought me back after the Raven Queen gave me her blessings," Ront defended.

"But he was there," Kriv said. "Giving me a guiding hand to freedom."

"Either way, man or woman, I'm just happy you're okay," Torinn said, wiping his cheek again. "Now I need you to go back home, Kriv. Your wife and the girls, you need to get them—"

"Dad," Kriv stopped him. Lerissa now clasped her hand over her mouth and began to cry.

"B—but how? Why?" Torinn choked out. You could hear the knot in his throat quickly forming.

"They were ruthless, father. They took them away before I could even understand what was going on," Kriv said, fighting his own emotions.

There wasn't a dry eye at the table. Everyone began to feel the emotions racing through Torinn.

"Where did they take them?" Torinn muttered from behind his teeth. Mr. R handed him a folded piece of cloth. He read it and smashed it in his hand. "I incinerate the note in my fist."

"What did it say?" I asked.

"We need to go to the Southlands," Torinn grumbled, pursing his lips in anger.

"Then we'd better hurry!" Rolen stated. "If they found us here, who knows how fast they might find us again!"

"Let's get a move on then," I said. "I make my way into the trees."

FIVE
SHORTCOMINGS

"WHAT'RE YOU DOING?" ROLEN YELLED. BUT I WAS already set on my path.

"I'm off to the Southlands!" I shouted back. Trying to make it sound as if I was actually getting further away. "Are you coming?"

Lerissa dragged her hand across her face. "We'd better go after him," she sighed. "Before he gets us killed."

"But I also have a teleport spell," Rolen said. "Get him back here and let's just teleport there."

"And who wants to tell the dwarf we have a better plan?" Lerissa asked sarcastically.

"This isn't the time to play games to make him feel better about himself!" Rolen complained. "Everyone's lives are at stake here!"

"Then we'd better get a move on," Lerissa told him. "And I take off after Adrik."

"What about Kriv?" Gimble asked. "Is he coming with us—"

"No," Torinn interrupted. "I can not risk his life for my mistakes. He must stay here and defend our home from these monsters should we fail." He turned to Mr. R. "Can you do that for me, Kriv?"

"No, let me go with you!" Kriv protested. "I can't just sit around while my girls are missing."

"You have to." Torinn raised his voice. "If I am to fall, you are my last line of defense. My first priority will be to get your girls back safely before anything else. I promise!"

"I understand," Kriv said. "I will defend Dracomear with my life." He bowed his head.

"You will defend this plane with your life," Torinn corrected him.

"Yes, father," Kriv nodded, keeping his head bowed.

"Okay, we need to get going," Ront chimed in. "We're going to end up finding Adrik's corpse in the forest if we don't hurry and catch up with him."

"Let's go," Torinn said.

"You all take off after Adrik into the forest around you," Mr. R began. "Following the footsteps you find printed into the soil from your heavy barbarian friend. We're going to visit Adrik who is much farther ahead of you all. Jack," Mr. R pointed to me. "What happens on your little march through the forest?"

"I'm thrashing my axe around. Smashing into trees and stumps. Just trying to hit something today," I explained.

"Okay. You all easily follow him through the carnage of partially destroyed trees," Mr. R said. "Now, Adrik, I need a perception check."

I rolled. "Seventeen."

"Through the smashing and mutilating of the forest, you hear a growling noise, much like a bear, followed by the echo of an owl's hoot." Mr. R described.

"I stop and ready my axe," I told him.

"The mixed animal noises begin to get closer and louder." Mr.

R clicked his keyboard and the noise began to play. It was odd. The bear growled, and the owl always hooted at the same time in the bear's growl. Like they were actually conjoined sounds.

"I stay still and tighten my grip on the axe," I explained.

"As you prepare for an attack, you watch as a brown-feathered bear-like creature breaches through the trees." Mr. R clicked his keyboard and an image of the owlbear come on the screen.

"Does it notice me?" I asked.

He rolled behind his screen. "It doesn't seem to have any concerns about you, but it has noticed you," he explained.

"I'm going to slowly put my axe away, and then sit quietly on the ground where I'm at," I described.

"Really?" Liam blurted. "You're gonna take the calm approach?"

"What am I supposed to do?" I defended. "It could probably eat me in a single bite. So I'm just gonna sit here and hope that I don't get eaten."

"As you calmly lay your arms down and take your seat, the owlbear begins to move towards you curiously," Mr. R narrated. "Inching a bit closer, trying to understand what you are. Until it's right in your face. Its humid, disgusting breath is blasting you in the face."

"I maintain my calm," I said.

"It begins to bump you and rub against you. Pecking you here and there, trying to get a reaction out of you."

"I carefully raise my hand and try to pet it on its neck."

"As you make contact with the soft feathers, the owlbear retreats a little out of fear. Roll me an animal handling."

I rolled my d20. "Sixteen?"

"The owlbear cautiously moves back towards you," Mr. R said.

"I'm gonna reach into my bag and offer it a little snack. Maybe some bread or something."

"You pull out a piece of bread from your bag and hold it out in your palm. The owlbear moves in to smell the bread before snatching it out of your hand and eating it," Mr. R described.

"I move in to pet it again."

"It eyes you as you move closer. Keeping its caution about you. But it doesn't retreat when you make contact. It even begins to nuzzle into your hand, guiding you on where to pet it."

"I pull out more bread and offer it."

"It inhales the bread, and then starts trying to root through your pack."

"No, no, no. You can't have it all," I scolded. "I need to eat that."

"It doesn't listen and forces itself into your bag," Mr. R said.

"I start pushing back against it."

"Roll me a strength saving throw," Mr. R asked.

"Twenty-one," I replied.

"You're managing to keep it at bay," he said before rolling his dice. "But you see anger growing in its eyes, and it knocks you backward."

"Okay, now would be a great time for you guys to find me." I sarcastically smiled.

"They are still far behind you," Mr. R assured me. "At this point, you are pinned to the ground by the massive owlbear that is rummaging through your bag."

"Can I try to get it off me?" I asked.

"Give me another strength saving throw with disadvantage since you're restrained."

"Eleven and twenty-seven," I sighed.

"You try to get the paw off your chest, but it doesn't budge," he said, rolling more dice. "And it's pushing down harder on your chest."

"Anytime now, you guys," I coughed out. "Maybe before my chest becomes a nice bowl for him to eat from."

Mr. R rolled some more. "Nope, they're still following your trail."

"I don't want to kill it," I whined. "Please don't make me kill it."

He rolled again. "Well, it finally found your rations." He chuckled. "And out of satisfaction, it gets off of your chest and sits back, gnawing on the meat it found in your pack."

"Now it's a test of dwarven morals," I contemplated. "Do I risk my life to be petty and keep my food? Or walk away before I get myself killed?"

"Don't be stupid," Liam sighed, shaking his head.

"Please let us find him," Laura pleaded. "For the sake of all that is good, let us find him."

Mr. R rolled a couple of times. A different expression for each roll. "You guys follow his path of destruction," he began. "And then it stops. And you hear the growling bear noises followed by the owl's hoot."

"You guys hold back," Ront said. "Let me scout ahead and make sure it's clear."

"Give me a perception check," Mr. R asked.

"Nineteen." Ront smiled.

"You move further into the forest, closer to the sounds of owls and bears. Until you break through into a small clearing where you come to a see..." Mr. R trailed off and pointed to me.

"Oh, umm," I hummed. "You find both an owlbear and Adrik attempting to eat the meat from my bag."

"Like the same piece?" Ront asked concerned.

"Yeah." I laughed. "Like dogs playing tug of war with a rope."

"Good lord," Ront sighed, slapping his face and dragging his hand down across it. "I'm gonna try to get his attention without alerting the owlbear." He cupped his hands around his mouth and whispered. "Adrik! Addy! Dumbass!"

Mr. R glared at him for a moment. "Adrik doesn't seem to hear you."

"I throw a rock at his head," Ront said.

"Roll to hit," Mr. R told him.

"What do I add?" Ront asked.

"Make it strength since you're throwing it at him," Mr. R smiled.

"Seventeen." Ront smirked back.

"You manage to hit him in the back of the head with a rock," Mr. R said.

"Ow!" I blurted. "The heck? Do I notice him?"

"Make me a perception check," Mr. R asked.

"Sixteen!" I declared.

"Yeah, you catch a glimpse of him in the trees behind you," Mr. R explained.

"What're you doing?" I whispered.

"What am *I* doing?" Ront asked defiantly. "What the hell are you doing?"

"Playing with an owlbear," I replied. "Are you guys really just catching up to me?"

"Well maybe if you would stop running off into the woods like an idiot, we could maybe find another way to the ruins besides hoofing it," Ront growled.

"Well, nobody was doing anything." I shrugged. "So I took the initiative and started moving us south."

Liam rolled his head to face his uncle. "Is he heading south?"

"Give me a nature check both of you," Mr. R smiled.

"Eleven," Ront said.

"Seventeen," I smirked, folding my arms and sitting back in my chair.

"Welp," Mr. R chuckled again. "From what you can gather he knows he's going south more than you really know."

"Lucky guess," Ront murmured. "What's the time of day look like?"

"You're inching at almost noon... at least from what you can tell from inside the trees," Mr. R said.

"So is everyone coming up behind you?" I whispered again to Liam.

"Are you insane?" Ront replied. "I'm not having them catch up with us while you're snacking with an owlbear. We're lucky that it hasn't noticed me and tried to maul you."

"You're overthinking this whole thing," I told him. Bringing my voice out of a whisper. "It's harmless. All it wanted was some food."

"You are insane." Ront shook his head. "So what's your plan here? We can't take an owlbear along with us."

"Why not?" I shrugged. "I bet Rolen would get along with it! Heck, he could talk to it."

"I swear you've lost it." Ront sighed.

"Just go get Rolen," I said, shooing him off. "Tell him I made a friend and he needs to meet them." I gave him a massive smile as I nodded for him to the group.

"I guess—I guess I go back and tell them what happened." Ront shook his head. "So it seems that Adrik, um, has, uh," he scratched the back of his head in thought. "Made friends with an owlbear?"

"You're kidding me?" Lerissa sighed pinching the bridge of her nose and shaking her head.

"Seriously?" Rolen asked, shocked.

"It appears so," Ront sighed.

"So now what?" Torinn questioned. "We can't just take on

an owlbear with us."

"He says Rolen can come talk to it," Ront said, pointing at Rolen.

"And what's that supposed to do?" Rolen asked.

"I—I don't know," Ront sighed.

"If it gets us moving to the Southlands then fine, I'll talk to the bear," Rolen groaned.

While they all discussed strategy on what to do about the bear and me, I wrote Mr. R a note.

Can I wrestle the bear?

Mr. R glanced over the note behind his screen and gave me a casual nod. He wrote something down and passed me back the piece of scrap paper.

Give me an athletics check.

I rolled my d20 as nonchalant as I could. I wrote my roll on the piece of paper.

24

He smirked and shook his head in surprise at my reply. But he didn't say no.

"I guess I'm going to talk to the bear," Rolen announced.

"As you go further into the woods following Ront, you hear the familiar sound of a bear growl followed by an owl's hoot. You come to a small break in the trees and there you see a massive owlbear on top of Adrik rolling around with him in its arms."

"Oh, you idiot," Ront shouted. "I draw my bow."

"No!" Rolen shouted. "Don't kill it! What if you hit Adrik? Or worse, what if that causes it to kill him?"

"It seems like it's already trying to." Ront fought back. "I'm gonna shoot it."

"Roll to hit," Mr. R said.

"Non-natural twenty," Ront divulged.

"You loose an arrow and it flies across the clearing and

buries itself into the owlbear's shoulder for..." he pointed to Liam.

"Seven piercing damage," Ront replied.

"It takes a moment for the owlbear to realize what just happened," Mr. R began. "It stops in its tracks and turns to look at the two of you."

"I nock another arrow," Ront said.

"The owlbear turns to charge you both," Mr. R said before rolling some dice. "And it runs at you both."

"I shoot again—" Ront started.

"Stop!" Rolen shouted. "I step between Ront and the owlbear and cast animal friendship."

"What's your spell DC?" Mr. R asked.

"Eighteen. And it's a wisdom saving throw," he replied.

"Well even if I rolled a twenty, the modifier is too negative to even attempt to combat that," Mr. R chuckled. "As Rolen steps between the drawn bow and the charging owlbear, you watch the angry owlbear stop just feet from plowing over Rolen and Ront, with its head cocked to the side."

"I slowly move closer, and then pet it," Rolen explained.

"You put your hand on its head and it nuzzles into your hand," Mr. R narrated.

"I sit down with it and cast speak with animals," Rolen said. "Can you understand me?" he asked.

"Uh huh!" the owlbear nodded. "I understand you."

"Good!" Rolen smiled. "Are you okay? Did my friend hurt you or scare you at all?"

"He glares at Ront," Mr. R explained.

"Ah yes, that's right," Rolen sighed. "I'm sorry about that, he's a bit jumpy. He doesn't understand nature. He doesn't realize you're just defending your home. But what about my other friend over there?" He motioned to me.

"No," the owlbear grumbled. "He my friend."

"Is he now?" Rolen said eyeing me. "And how did he become your friend?"

"He feed me," The owlbear replied. "And he play with me."

"Well, he's very good at both of those, now isn't he?" Rolen laughed.

"He not like bad people who attack me," the owlbear growled.

"Again, I'm sorry for him," Rolen said shooing off Liam.

"No," the owlbear grunted. "Other bad people."

"What do you mean other bad people?" Rolen asked raising his eyebrow.

"You watch as the owlbear moves its paw to reveal scars along its beak," Mr. R described. "Some still fresh and bloody."

"Do you remember what they look like?" Rolen asked, then turned to Ront and me. "Go get the others!"

"Metal people," the owlbear bellowed. "Black metal people."

"What were they doing out here? Do you remember?"

"They had a girl."

"A girl?" Rolen's voice peaked. "D—did she have ears like mine?"

Mr. R nodded. "They take her that way," he pointed with his head. "And you notice that it's directing you south."

"Was she alive?" Rolen asked, the concern growing in his voice.

Mr. R nodded again, slowly. "She not happy to go with metal people. Metal people make her stop fighting. I try to help girl... but too many metal people."

"It's okay," Rolen said. "You did your best, and that's all any of us could do."

"And as you say that, your friends come running through the trees," Mr. R narrated.

"Oh good," Rolen let out. "Tor, I need your help. My friend

here has an arrow in their shoulder and I need your help to heal them when I take it out."

"Are you crazy?" Torinn shouted. "That's an owlbear! You're gonna get mauled when you rip that out of him!"

"*They*," Rolen emphasized. "Understand what's about to happen. Just get ready. The less pain they can be in the better."

"Okay," Torinn nodded. "I lay my hands around the arrow wound and prepare to cast cure wounds once the arrow is out."

"Okay," Mr. R said. "The two of you move and place your hands around the wound, Rolen grabbing the arrow with his other hand."

"On three. One, two—three!" Rolen shouted as he mimed ripping an arrow out of a massive owlbear's shoulder.

Mr. R clicked his keyboard and a booming bear roar rang throughout the house followed by a high-pitched owl screech. "As you tear out the arrow with a schlurp, you feel the slight splash of blood on your faces before watching the wound completely heal itself shut," he described. "A little bit of dried blood being the only remains of the wound."

"You okay now?" Rolen asked.

Mr. R nodded somberly.

"It'll be okay, they can't hurt you anymore," Rolen assured.

"You start to hear the bear growl and hoot again like it did before," Mr. R explained.

"The spell ran out?" Rolen asked.

Mr. R nodded again.

"I want to reach into my bag and pull out the cabbage seeds," Rolen explained. "And I want to druidcraft them into full cabbages for our new friend."

"You hold these seeds in your palm and focus your arcane energy onto the seeds. And before your eyes, like watching a nature channel movie, these seeds rapidly grow into full heads of cabbage. Vibrant, green, and pungent. And the owlbear sits back eyeing the cabbages."

"I hand it one of the cabbages," Rolen said.

"It reaches out and takes it between its paws," Mr. R described. "Before tearing it to shreds and devouring every bite."

"I hand it the rest," Rolen smiled.

"Can we keep it?" I asked. "Come on you guys, please! I'll take care of it."

Lerissa laughed out loud before slapping her hands over her face. "I'm sorry," she said. "But an owlbear is a huge responsibility. And we don't want to endanger it going south—"

"Well," Rolen interrupted. "We might need it."

"Why do we need a huge owlbear?" Lerissa asked.

"It kind of saw a group of our friends who stopped your teleportation, dragging a girl behind them. A girl with my kind of ears," Rolen explained.

"Do you think it's her?" Gimble asked.

"It has to be!" Rolen replied. "What would Death's Hand be doing out here dragging away half-elven girls?"

"What would a half-elven girl be doing out here in the first place?" Ront questioned.

"Who knows?" Rolen defended. "But all I know is this has to be Elfi. If she wasn't important wouldn't they have just killed her and left the body here in the woods?"

"So what do we do?" I asked.

"Best we can do is continue down into the Southlands," Torinn said. "Even if they don't take Elfi there, we need to go and rescue Kriv's girls!"

SIX

TAKE FIVE

"AND THAT IS A GOOD SPOT TO STOP AND TAKE A BREAK," Mr. R said craning his neck and stretching his arms. He spun his chair and wheeled out of the room and into the kitchen.

"Great!" Daryl blurted out before darting out of the room behind Mr. R, presumably to the bathroom. Sometimes I'm surprised that he can make it through anything without peeing himself. Although, he did once go through a seventeen-hour Star Wars marathon without a break. Lost ten bucks on that too.

"Ahhh," Ben let out as he stretched up to the ceiling. "I've got my cards, Liam, quick game or two before we get back into it?"

Liam's eyes narrowed onto Ben. "Which cards?"

"Magic and Yu-Gi-Oh." Ben smiled.

"Make it interesting?" Liam grinned.

"Depends," Ben narrowed his gaze back at Liam.

"Best two out of three of Magic. Winner gets the Loser's best Yu-Gi-Oh monster," Liam explained. A kind of ominous smile grew across his face.

Ben thought for a second before reaching his hand out.

"Deal! It'll be nice to take that Blue-Eyes White Dragon off you."

"You wish," Liam joked.

"We'll see," Ben laughed. They walked off together through the doorway into the kitchen.

"So what do you think?" I heard Laura ask. I spun around to answer her... until I realized she was talking to Jake. She had her phone out in front of them.

"Cute," Jake said. "But I don't know. Not my style."

"Yeah, me neither." Laura laughed.

"Well hold on," Jake said as he moved his fingers against Laura's phone screen. "Who's that?"

"That's Sam." She laughed. "But..."

"He's not, huh?" Jake asked.

"Well," Laura's voice squeaked.

"Dang woman, is he or isn't he?" Jake interrogated.

"We don't actually know." She gave him a cheesy grin. "He hasn't exactly come out to anyone yet."

"Oh, I understand," Jake nodded. "He's shy?"

"Oh no," Laura laughed. "Most confident person I've ever met. But his parents—"

"Are against it." Jake sighed.

"No," She shook her head and smiled. "They just really badly want grandkids. He just is too afraid to tell them that he might never deliver that."

"Well, why don't you get Mr. Sam here out for drinks one night and introduce us?" Jake laughed.

"You sure you're up for that?" Laura asked.

"Yeah?" he replied skeptically. "Why? Wouldn't be the first man I've helped walk out of the dreaded closet. Besides, it's not like he's freakishly deformed, right? Like, I can handle an extra toe or third nipple, but if he's hiding an ingrown twin on his stomach or something, then give a man a heads up."

"No," Laura blurted out laughing. She laughed so hard, she snorted! She clapped her hands over her mouth. After a minute or two of fighting the urge not to laugh, she moved her hands and wiped away the tears. "None of that! No, he's just crazy smart."

"Like trivia smart?" Jake awkwardly grinned.

"More like musical prodigy studying to be a neurosurgeon with a huge interest in astronomy and physics," Laura returned the awkward grin.

"Oh," Jake replied. "And I just thought he was attractive... but hey, you can only try right?"

"I guess you're right." Laura laughed again. "So tomorrow sound good?"

"I get out of work with Ma at three. So as long as I can grab a shower we're good," Jake explained.

"Alright, I'll go call him real quick and see if he's down," Laura said as she walked into the kitchen.

Jake shook his head and smiled, staring at the ground. He started towards the kitchen but stopped when he noticed I was the only one left in the room.

"Oh, Jack... I didn't see you there," he told me through an embarrassed smile.

"So..." I said staring at him expressionlessly. "On a scale of Steve Buscemi to Channing Tatum... how cute was he?" I asked, breaking the awkward tension with a smile to let him know I was messing with him.

"Ahh, you're funny, kid." He laughed, pointing at me. "Ya know if I had to put him on that scale..." He stopped to think for a second. "I'd rank him a John Cho."

My face must have been motionless and more expressionless than before because his jaw dropped.

"Oh come on man!" He said, shocked. "Ya know, Harold and Kumar? The stoner movie from like two thousand four?"

I just shrugged. "Dude, I was still learning how to function as a living human being in two thousand four."

"Man, I'd have thought your mom would've shown it to you by now," he said. "That was one of your Dad's favorite movies. Might have been on account that it was one of the first things your parents went out and did after you were born. They locked themselves away for months after you came around. They wanted nothing to do with anything if it didn't involve watching you with a video camera." He chuckled. "They even hired me and Matt to come watch you that night. They thought it better if we were both there. That way you were never alone without someone to watch you." He leaned in a little closer. "But between us both, I think they just didn't trust the military trainee with a poop bomb." He smiled at me and grabbed my shoulder. He gave me a tight squeeze as his eyes began to water.

"I know," I smiled. "I miss him too."

"He was a good man, Jack. A good man taken from us far too early," Jake assured me fighting back tears. "I just wish he could see what an amazing young man you're growing up to be. He'd be so proud. A little spooked at how much you look like him, but proud as all hell!" He sniffed. "Although he might be a little disappointed."

I felt my smile dropped into an expression of confusion. "How come?" I asked him.

"You haven't seen Harold and Kumar! What about Wayne's World? You have to have seen that?" He questioned.

I shook my head.

"Dude, we gotta change that." He pulled out his phone and began typing and reading aloud. "Required movies to make father proud. Harold and Kumar go to White Castle, Wayne's World, Harold and Kumar Escape from Guantanamo Bay, and Wayne's World Two. Oh, and also any Mel Brooks movies. He loved those."

"Yeah, Blazing Saddles was his favorite," I stated.

"Okay, so maybe he would be proud." Jake chuckled giving me a wink. We sat there for a moment awkwardly smiling before his stomach broke the silence and awkward laughter with a loud gurgle. "Oh man," he said. "I need to get some pizza in there. Come on, I know you could use another slice too."

I got up from my chair and stretched every muscle I could before following behind Jake.

"No!" I heard Ben shout. "That's not how that works!"

"You're just mad that it means you lose," Liam argued back.

"No!" Ben repeated. "If the monster is tapped it can't block."

"He wasn't tapped," Liam defended.

"He was sideways and you turned him when I declared attackers," Ben fought. "You're supposed to untap during your upkeep otherwise you can't untap!"

"So I forgot to during my upkeep. It would have been untapped either way. But it doesn't matter. I won, you lost, pay up." Liam smiled. "I believe you owe me a Magician of Black Chaos." He held his hand out to Ben.

"What? No way!" Ben shouted. "You cheated! I'm not rewarding cheating."

"Fine," Liam shrugged. "I'll duel you for it." He grinned, pulling up a card from his pocket and holding it in his two fingers with the black and bronze swirling back facing everyone else. "That is, if you're not chicken," he mocked.

"Nobody calls me chicken," Ben recited. He reached into his pocket and pulled out a deck of similar cards, shuffling them in his hand. "I believe in the heart of the cards," he quoted.

"Let's duel!" Liam shouted.

"Hold up," Laura interrupted, her mouth still full of pizza. "I play winner." She smiled. "Same stakes."

"Well, I hope you're ready to lose to me and my soon-to-be Magician of Black Chaos." Liam snickered.

"Please," Ben laughed. "Even if you end up beating me, you think you've got a chance against her? You can't even beat me fairly."

"What, are you afraid of your sister?" Liam mocked him again.

"No, I'm just saying. If you beat me and play her, I'll just end up with my card back," Ben explained.

"We'll see," Liam grinned.

I pushed my way around the two dueling and went over to the pizza, pulled out a slice, and turned to watch the game.

Laura came and stood beside me. "So, who are we thinking here?" she asked.

"Well, let's see," I stalled. I wasn't paying attention to who had what in their deck and didn't actually know who was doing what. But before I could even get my answer out...

"Lights out!" Ben shouted. "Dark Magician Girl attacks your Beaver Warrior, destroying it and draining your remaining eight-hundred life points. I win!"

"I'm gonna guess, Ben," I joked.

"Well, I'll be." Laura laughed. "I didn't think he had it in him," she whispered.

"That'll be one Blue-Eyes White Dragon please," Ben gloated with his hand out.

"Alright," Liam rolled his eyes. He sifted through his cards and pulled out one and handed it to Ben. "You bested me."

Ben took the card and then shook Liam's hand. "GG my friend. GG."

"Yeah, good game," Liam said, defeated. "But I'll get that card back."

"I'll hold you to that." Ben laughed. "You ready, Laura?"

"It's time to d—d—duel!" Laura blurted. She pulled out a

deck of cards from her back pocket and began shuffling it in her hands. Ben flipped a coin, caught it, and slapped it on the top of his hand.

"Tails," Laura called.

Ben moved his hands a revealed the coin. It was heads.

"I think I'll go second." She smiled at him.

As they drew their first hand, I felt my phone vibrate in my pocket. It was Mom. I grabbed a second slice of pizza and another plate and went into the game room to answer the phone.

"Hey!" I answered.

"Hey baby," Mom answered back. "How's the game going?"

"Not bad," I told her. "Lots of story so far. We burnt a library down, I made friends with an owlbear, we killed a guy. Nothing unusual. How's work going?"

"For a Friday night, it's kinda slow." She sighed. "But I can't complain. It'll pick up real soon. Everyone's out eating now, so they'll be here in the next hour or so. At least I hope." She laughed.

"I bet people will show," I assured her. "It's Friday night, people are looking to forget the long work week."

She laughed. "I hope you're right. Anyways, where are you guys off to?"

"The Southland Ruins," I told her. "We're tracking Death's Hand there. They might have Elfi down there."

"Oh, so you guys found her?" Her voice sounded excited.

"Not entirely," I chuckled. "So far we're not one hundred percent certain if it's her. We know they have a half-elven girl. But they also have three dragonborn women. Torinn's grandchildren and daughter-in-law. So it might be someone being held as hostage against something else. But I have a feeling it's her. Why would it not be? She's a huge part of this story arc."

"Who knows, maybe it's a red herring," she said. "Something to distract you guys from what's really going on."

"I never thought of that," I responded. "Maybe you're right."

"Well duh." She laughed. "I'm your mom, of course I am." I could feel her snarky grin through the phone.

"Yeah, until you need tech support." She could probably feel me returning the snarky grin back at her through the phone. Just one of those genetic traits I managed to get from her instead of dad.

"Ha, ha, mister funny," she jokingly mocked. "Ask for help restarting your computer one time. Anyways, what are you guys up to? I'm guessing you're on break since you answered the phone."

"Yeah, we are. I'm pretty sure Jake and Mr. R went to do their usual shop talk in the garage. Plan their next big project. Daryl ran off to the bathroom. Ben just beat Liam in a wager match of Yu-Gi-Oh and is now playing against his sister. And I'm talking to you," I explained.

"Well, that's good," she said. "What are they playing for?"

"Who, Ben and Liam? They're playing for each other's cards. Winner gets the loser's best card. But I'm pretty sure Laura is hustling them and returning their cards."

"She's such a sweetheart."

"She's pretty cool," I agreed.

"Well hey, I've got to start heading back to work. Before these invisible people start raiding the bar. Text me when you're on your way home. Maybe if we're heading back at the same time we could go get some late night pie or something?" She asked.

"Oh yeah!" I replied. "I could do pie."

"Well then let's get pie after everything." She laughed.

"Let's hope I can make some tips here though, otherwise you're gonna have to buy," she joked.

"As long as I get some pie, I'm cool," I assured her.

"Well I'll let you go then." She sighed. "Love you, kiddo."

"Love you too, Mom," I reminded her. "Good luck tonight, I know you're gonna get a boom of people."

"Thanks, baby. Good luck on finding Elfi." She laughed again. "See you later."

"Bye, Mom," I said before hanging up.

"Hey, pie boy," Daryl said from the doorway.

I signed back at him. *Were you eavesdropping?*

What? Me? You're nuts man! I'm deaf, I can't eavesdrop, He joked, tapping on his implants behind his ear.

Don't lie to me, I joked back. *I know it's all a ruse. Really you're just wearing those to get special treatment.*

You caught me. Guys, the jig is up, He laughed. "But really, I'm pretty much deaf. Why can't people understand that?" His heavy diction breaking through the silence.

"Don't let it get to you," I said. "She was a sub who doesn't realize she's not the only person in the world."

"Yeah," he chuckled. "But next time you wanna talk across the room like that, don't be so obvious. Or just don't do it during a test."

"Who? Me?" I replied, pretending to be offended. "I would never, ever, ever, try to get you to give me answers through some kind of hand code that nobody understands anymore. I mean come on, it's a dead form of communication, like morse code. Just ask her. She knew everything."

We both laughed for a good minute before wiping away tears and trying to breathe. I grabbed my inhaler out of my bag and took a huge puff.

"Easy there," Daryl said. "You okay?"

"Yeah, yeah, I'm good," I assured him. "All good!" I gave him a thumbs up before bending over to cough a bit. "All good," I repeated through the coughs.

"Okay," he responded skeptically. "Come grab some water or something."

I nodded and gave him another thumbs up. He left the room and I followed behind him a minute later.

As I walked into the kitchen I saw everyone now around the center island. Liam, Ben, Jake, and Laura were all holding a hand of cards. From what I gathered it was a four man duel. Mr. R was on the side watching. I'm guessing more as a judge rather than a spectator.

"I special summon my Dark Magician," Laura announced. "I discard my Alligator's Sword and Crass Clown cards. And then I attack Liam!"

"My turn," Liam squinted as he drew a card from his deck. "I sacrifice my Dragon Zombie and King of Yamimakai and summon Blue-Eyes White Dragon! I attack your Dark Magician, destroying it him and dealing the remaining five-hundred damage directly at you!"

"Dang," Laura nodded in approval. "Guess I didn't have what it takes for a two-v-two. Good luck, bud." She laughed slapping Jake on the back.

"I play my Black Magic Ritual card and summon Magician of Black Chaos." Jake announced as he placed two cards on the counter. "I then cast an equip spell, the Gravity Axe Grarl. I equip it to my magician. That raises his attack to three thousand five hundred after adding the Yami spell card from earlier."

Liam's smile of victory quickly dropped when he realized what was coming.

"I attack your Blue-Eyes White Dragon. Dealing a residual blow of five-hundred to you. Taking you out." Jake laughed maniacally.

"What the hell!" Liam shouted, blinking at the cards. "How

the hell?" He stammered trying to gather his words. "When did you get good at this?"

"When I tell you that we got bored on base between training and patrol, we get really good at things like this," he reminded Liam. "They didn't even know what was coming at them when I was stationed in Afghanistan. They set me down with their best player and I destroyed him in four turns... twice."

"Well let's see if that confidence will hold up," Ben said as he drew a card. He paused for a moment and then set his cards down. "Yeah, never mind. You win." He surrendered. "You are the ultimate master of the house."

Liam and Ben knelt down on the floor and began bowing to Jake.

"We're not worthy! We're not worthy!" They chanted together.

Jake shot me a look. "See, they know Wayne's World."

"Well, now I guess I have to see it," I joked. "I take it that was an interesting game?"

"Quick one," Laura answered.

"Eh, she's just mad that I beat her," Liam gloated.

"But my team won," she defended.

"But you were the first one out," Ben teased.

"Still on the winning team," Laura fought back.

"Can we all just agree Jake is the true winner here?" Daryl interrupted the teasing.

"I can agree to that," Mr. R said. "So now that we have discovered the best amongst us, shall we get back to our game?"

"Let's do it," Jake cheered. "We've got women to find and save!" he shouted as he ran into the front room with his index finger extended high above his head.

"Hey, Jack, would you go grab a container of those treats Wade brought over?" Mr. R asked as he headed into the game room.

"Sure," I nodded. I started for the garage when I heard Laura in the kitchen.

"I'll go give him a hand." Her footsteps seemed to boom in my head as she got closer. And then she was standing in front of me. "Ya gonna open the door there?"

"W—what? Oh right," I stuttered. I swung the door open. "After you," I said gesturing towards the open door.

"Why thank you." She laughed.

I followed behind her. I walked down the small set of stairs and turned towards the freezer, where I was met by a bent over Laura. I froze in my tracks.

"What am I looking for again?" she asked.

"C—c—cannoli." My voice cracked. I tugged on my collar. It was getting hot. Or maybe it was just me. I avoided staring as best I could but she was bent over in front of me in the way of where I'm supposed to be looking. What am I supposed to do?

"I'm not seeing them. You remember where you put them in here? " she asked.

"Th—they're in the backside—" I stopped myself. "In the back." What is the matter with me? I see her every week. Why do I get all flustered and awkward around her?

"Found them!" She shouted from inside the freezer.

"Oh thank god!" I sighed out.

She stood up and turned to me, handing me a container. "You okay? You look a little flushed." She reached out and placed her hand on my forehead. "You're burning up. Do you feel sick?"

"N—no, no!" I lied. "I feel great. Just a little warm in here that's all."

"You sure?" she interrogated. "Because I'm freezing!" She said folding her arms across her chest.

I slammed my eyes shut. This was all just a bad nightmare coming true. Or was it a dream come true? Alone with Laura?

No, what? Stop thinking that! She's older than you! You're still just a kid! It's not even legal! I've heard of too many YouTube celebrities get in trouble for having a relationship with under-aged kids. And it ruined them. I couldn't do that to Laura to live out a lifetime dream. She's too amazing.

"But seriously, are you okay?" She interrupted my thoughts. "You've been standing there with your eyes shut for an entire minute now."

I opened my eyes again. There she still stood. The red and yellow contact lenses threw me off for a second. I forgot she still had them on. But it didn't detract from her gorgeous face!

"Hello? Jack?" She waved at my face. "You in there?"

"W—what? Oh yeah. I'm here," I lied again. "It was that weird mid-sneeze thing where your body goes to sneeze but never actually does and you just sit there looking like an idiot waiting."

"Okay?" She eyed me as if I was an escaped mental patient.

"Trust me, I'm okay," I assured her. "Let's get these back inside before they get warm." And I turned and walked back into the house.

I didn't look back out of fear I might freeze up again. I went straight to the game room and opened the container.

"Cannoli anyone?" I asked offering the container. Mr. R reached over and grabbed one. As well as Jake and Liam.

"Rainbow cookie or pizzelle?" I heard Laura ask behind me. For some reason that sent chills down my back and my hair stood on end. Daryl reached over my shoulder and grabbed a cookie from Laura.

"These are really good!" Jake said through a mouth full of cannoli. "Where'd these come from again?"

"Kurtis sent them," I told him. "He's expanding the restaurant into a bakery according to Wade."

"No way?" Jake asked surprised. "That's awesome. These

are really good. Might have to swing by there and get one of these for Mom," he said to Daryl.

"She'd love these," Daryl agreed.

"Awesome, so now that we have sweets in our mouths, you guys ready to continue?" Mr. R asked, swallowing a huge bite of cannoli. Like a team, we all nodded in agreement. Still stuffing our faces with sweets. "Great. Then let's begin."

SEVEN

LIVING THE NIGHTMARES

Mr. R clapped his hands together and rubbed them back and forth. "Let's jump back into the story," he said. He rummaged through a couple of papers and wrote a few things down before looking back up at us. "You guys were just about to make your way towards the Southland Ruins when Adrik encountered an owlbear who turned out to have information that aided your adventure."

"And it's now our companion," I noted.

"Yes." Mr. R chuckled. "For the time being, they are your companion."

"Is it at all possible to ride it?" I asked. "Considering I'm only like four and a half feet tall."

"Oh yeah!" Gimble agreed. "Me too!"

"Yeah," Mr. R contemplated. "I guess you guys could ride it. That would slow it down a bit because Adrik is still pretty heavy as a dwarf. And he has some heavy weaponry."

"Okay, maybe I won't then," I sighed.

"Can I still do it without slowing it?" Gimble asked.

Mr. R thought for a moment. Rolled a few dice. "Yeah, you

can ride. You're small enough and traveling light enough that it will manage to maintain its speed with you."

"Awesome!" he cheered. "Then I'm going to ride!"

"Alright. What's the marching order?" Mr. R asked.

"I think it would be smart for us to have Rolen lead," Lerissa said. "I'll walk ahead with him. But I think having the nature boy guide us would be the smartest idea."

"I agree," Rolen joined. "I have the best chance of safely guiding us out of this forest." He turned back to face Mr. R. "Relative to Dracomear, how close are the Ruins?"

"Dracomear is the southernmost kingdom on the continent of Tanear. And much like Spain and Morocco, Tanear and the southern continent of Seartia are separated by a small body of water. No more than maybe forty-five kilometers wide," Mr. R explained.

"So we're close?" Rolen asked.

"Relatively." Mr. R shrugged. "Maybe another day or two of travel on foot."

"Then we should maybe set up camp for the night," Rolen said. "I doubt we make it much further than here for the night. How far did we make it?"

"After just going straight south through this dense forest for what was the majority of the afternoon and some of the early evening, as you talk about setting camp for the night, you break from the tree line and find yourself atop a very large cliff side., Mr. R described. "And below at the bottom of the cliff sits a large desert. And quite a ways out lies a large city. Far in the distance, but visible by its size."

"Well," Rolen started. "Camp here and then head into the city out there tomorrow?"

"Why can't we go there now?" I asked. "It's right there."

"We don't know what that town is," Lerissa reminded me. "And remember last time we went into a town at night? We drew an undead monster to a powerful wizard's home and ended up getting him killed. Do we want to do that again?"

"I guess not," I sighed.

"So we're setting up here?" Torinn asked.

"Yeah," Rolen replied.

"Well, Gimble," Lerissa turned to him. "Mind opening up our camp?"

"Sure thing." Gimble smiled. "I whip out my violin and bust out *Welcome to My House*."

"You guys watch as Gimble pulls out his violin and begins to play a new tune you don't recognize. The arcane door begins to swirl into existence in the trunk of a nearby tree," Mr. R described. "And the doors swing in revealing the familiar mansion inside."

"I head in and go straight to my room," Lerissa said.

"Me too," Rolen joined. "I'm going to meditate again."

"I'm going to relax in the parlor." Gimble chuckled. "Relax, maybe read a book or two."

"And the rest of you?" Mr. R asked.

"I would like to go down to the meditation, hot spring room thing that we made up a while back," Ront said.

"I would like to retire to my quarters for a while," Torinn narrated.

"I wanna take our new friend the owlbear into a room that would make it comfortable. Maybe bring it some food," I explained. "Maybe something woodland- like. Similar to Rolen's room."

"I create that room for him next to his room," Gimble said.

"You all hear a muffled thunk, as a new room erupts from the walls down the hall," Mr. R described.

"Thanks," I told Gimble.

"Anytime. After you feed the bear, want to grab our usual drink from the cellar?" Gimble asked.

"Is that even a question?" I joked.

"I'll hold ya to that. And I walk inside," Gimble narrated.

"Me too," I said.

"Alright. As you all make your way to your respective rooms for the evening, Ront, Torinn, and Rolen, I would like you to run me through what you're up to." Mr. R requested.

"I set up my usual meditation ritual," Rolen started without skipping a beat. "The incense burning beside me as I sit on the tree stump in the middle of my room."

"Okay," Mr. R nodded. "And you two?"

"I am praying to Pelor before I retire for the night," Torinn said.

"I am getting down into my skivvies and taking a dip in the hot spring. Clear my head and meditate," Ront explained.

"Alright, can I get all three of you to make me a wisdom saving throw," Mr. R asked.

"Twenty," Rolen called out.

"Twenty also," Ront replied.

"Twenty-eight," Torinn joined.

"Okay," Mr. R nodded again. "The three of you each as you close your eyes and fall into the serenity of meditation. You begin to feel like you're floating, set adrift in the darkness of nothing. As you open your eyes again, you find yourself floating in the same darkness, almost like you never opened your eyes."

"Hello?" Ront asked.

"All three of you hear Ront's voice echo through the darkness.

"Ront? Is that you?" Torinn added.

"And his voice echoes through the dark," Mr. R repeated.

"Where are we?" Rolen joined.

"And as you all hear Rolen's voice echo through the darkness, a blast of fire lights up the darkness and surrounds you all. Each one of you seeing a different color of flame. For Ront, the flames burn a deep purple. Torinn, your flames burn with an orange amber hue. And Rolen, your flames burn with a somber green." Mr. R described. "As you all look around, you notice that you three are right beside each other."

"What is this?" Rolen asked.

"I'm guessing it's another divine meeting," Torinn responded.

"Then why is he here?" Ront questioned.

"Good question," Torinn agreed.

"As you ask this, a face appears, floating above the three of you. A familiar face to one of you..." Mr. R began. He clicked his keyboard and the image of the Mind Flayer appeared again.

"Oh this isn't good," Rolen sighed.

"Cease your search immediately or suffer a punishment worse than death," the Illithid threatened. "Leave us the girl and we will return your loved ones," he scowled. "And then hanging in the air amongst the flames are four female bodies... and one male."

"No," Rolen whispered. "No, no, no, no!" Each no gaining volume. "Not this again!" He buried his face into his hands.

"What is this?" Ront asked.

"It's the nightmare all over again," Rolen explained. "But this time they're not talking about killing you guys! It wasn't you guys at all!"

"What do you mean it wasn't us?" Torinn interrogated.

"I lied about the last nightmare," Rolen confessed. "I had this same kind of dream, the five hanging bodies! But now... Now I know who they really are gonna hurt."

"And what if we don't cease?" Torinn asked Mr. R.

"We will destroy those that you love, but be torturing them to the brink of death in front of your eyes. Only to let them wilt away in your arms as you try to tell them everything will be okay." Mr. R smiled.

"You don't frighten us," Torinn fought back. "I have lived long enough to know when someone threatens me or my family, it's because they are afraid of what I am."

"You are a fool, Torinn Yarjerit," the Illithid growled. "You believe you are powerful as you hide behind that crest upon your chest. Imagine the power you could have if you were to join us." He turned to look at Ront. "Just look how our goddess has treated your companion. Imagine what she could do for you."

"I do not shudder at the evil of your cult. And neither does Pelor!" Torinn claimed. "And I will defend this plane and the next from the evils you spew. For I have seen the light through her divine grace. You shall fall by my hand at her will!"

"Then you... shall... die!" the Illithid shouted. "And with that Torinn is impaled by a shadow spike through his chest."

"Argh!" Torinn screamed, looking down at his chest. "Oh, mighty, Pelor! Give me the graces of your might... so I may send them back into the light," Torinn scowled.

"And with this call to the goddess on high, you all notice Torinn's armor begin to shine bright white. His eyes glaze over and his yellow irises transform to a solid white glow. Arcane energy misting from his eyes," Mr. R described. "His body begins to rise in the air from the shadow spike. A pair of bright white angel wings sprout from his back. And from Torinn's mouth, you hear a prominent female's voice, echoed by multiple other, deeper, more booming voices.

Your reign is coming to an end! Your army shall be defeated. Your tower shall fall! You are no match for my champion! Death's Hand is done!" He clicked his keyboard and the screen flashed white. And there appeared an image of the goddess herself. Pelor. "You all watch as, from Torinn's body, a blast of arcane energy lights up the room, turning the dark abyss into a plane of white. And from Torinn's body, that is now floating back down to the ground, Pelor emerges from his chest. Like a spirit leaving the body."

"I drop to a knee and bow before her," Ront said. "Your Greatness."

"Thank you, my child," Pelor said acknowledging the welcome.

"W—why? W—what is happening?" Rolen stammered.

"Your companion has called upon me," Pelor assured. "In his dire need, he called upon me to aid you in a time of need."

"But this isn't any danger yet," Rolen stated. "This is only a vision. Arcane tricks, illusions, fake."

"That may be my child," Pelor replied somberly. "But these are powerful arcane illusions." He gestured to Torinn. "You all turn your attention to Torinn, who is now lying on the white floor, seizing on the ground. His eyes are solid black. The veins in his neck bulging and discolored. His lips are growing blue and the red scales on his face are fading to a paler shade. A black liquid spilling from his mouth. You recognize these symptoms. This spell you have seen before."

"No!" Ront shouted.

"This is the same effect you've seen used by Death's Hand's soldiers after a failed mission," Pelor explained. "He is suffering. And from you, Torinn, I need a constitution saving throw."

"Twenty," he said.

"Okay. You take thirty-six points of necromancy damage," Mr. R told him.

"So what do we do to save him?" Rolen asked. The fear peaking in his voice.

"The pain will pass," Pelor assured him. His voice returning to its female tone. "But a little part of him will die inside. This magic is not to be taken lightly. These perversions of the elements and the natural order are dangerous."

"So what do we do?" Ront asked. "What are we supposed to do to fight this? We are not equipped to combat this."

"You must become equipped." He sighed. "For there is not much more we could ask of you. If there were more time, maybe. But by the looks of my champion... there isn't enough."

"Then what must we do?" Ront began to grow angrily impatient. "Anything! Just tell us!"

"Continue your journey to the Ruins. Learn what they have planned. And stop it at all costs," Pelor explained.

"What are they planning?" Rolen asked.

"We aren't sure." He sighed in defeat. "The darkness has clouded our ability to observe them anymore. But we do know there is a massive amount of dark energy being used in the Southlands. Beyond anything we have ever seen."

"So it's hopeless either way?" Rolen sighed, slumping his shoulders.

"You're giving up?" Ront asked.

"What can we do?" Rolen responded. "They're more powerful than anything we have ever fought. I mean come on, Reita managed to kill one of us."

"And right now they're killing another one," Ront gestured to Torinn.

"Oh my god! Torinn!" Rolen shouted. "I drop next to him and try to shake him from this."

"As you pick him off the ground, and feel him struggle to breathe, Pelor reaches her hand down to your shoulder. The warm feeling contrasts dramatically with the cold dragonborn in your arms." Mr. R described. "You need to let him go," Pelor told Rolen.

"Let him go?" Rolen repeated. "Let him go? He's not dead! He's still breathing! I can hear it!"

"And as you say that, Torinn's body begins grow pale," Mr.

R said. "Torinn, any final words?"

"Save... the girls," Torinn forced out.

"And with that, Torinn falls limp in your arms," Mr. R said.

"No... No! No! No!" Rolen sobbed. "No! He can't... You can't!" He shouted pointing at Mr. R. Tears welling in his eyes. "This isn't fair! He was your champion! Bring him back! We need him! The world needs him! Take me instead!"

"Rolen," Pelor looked at him. "Rolen, you both need to wake up."

"What?" Rolen asked.

"Wake up," Pelor repeated.

"I wake up," Ront said.

"And Rolen, you watch as Ront's body collapses and withers away," Mr. R narrated.

"I—I wake up," Rolen said skeptically.

"You feel a rushing energy come over you. And in a blur, you're thrown back into your body. Still sitting on your stump. Incense barely burnt," Mr. R explained.

"I run to Torinn's room," Rolen said.

"You blast your way out of your room and barrel down the hallway towards Torinn's room. Running through the servants and pushing past moving items. You make your way into his room," Mr. R directed. "And there on the floor, gasping for air is Torinn. Blinking back into existence."

"Oh thank the gods!" Rolen cheered. "I drop down to help him sit up. A—are you okay?" he asked Torinn.

"I don't know how they administer that spell to themselves willingly," Torinn painfully joked. "But am I okay?" he asked Mr. R.

"You're alive," Mr. R began. "But you are bleeding from your chest. And when you remove the armor to examine the wound... there is a decent sized hole in your chest that goes all the way through to you back."

"I want to cast cure wounds on myself," he muttered.

"You focus your arcane energy from your amulet. The warm glow and essence of Pelor surging through your body. As the wound begins to close itself. A slight tinge of pain shoots through you as the wound stretches and pulls itself shut," Mr. R depicted.

"That was some dream." Torinn laughed. "Help me onto my bed?"

"Yeah," Rolen nodded. "I help him into the bed."

"I come join them once I can," Ront added. "Bringing Lerissa with me."

"Do you wake up and go with him?" Mr. R asked Lerissa.

"Well, I'm guessing he came in with some form of urgency." Lerissa shrugged. "I go."

"You both come rushing into Torinn's chambers where you find a very weak Torinn being helped into his bed by a shaken Rolen. And a nasty scar adorning Torinn's back side," Mr. R illustrated.

"W—what happened?" Lerissa asked shocked. Her hand over her mouth.

"Oh it was nothing," Torinn assured her. "Just an arcane mishap." He chuckled, and then let out a grunt of pain. "Nothing I can't heal away."

"Are you crazy, old man?" Ront blurted out. "You died! We watched you die!"

"What are you talking about?" Lerissa shot at Ront. "How did he almost die? Where were you three?"

"It was another—" Rolen began.

"Death's Hand knows were after them," Torinn interrupted. "They have my girls and Elfi... and another, but I'm not too sure who they were. But this wasn't just a dream or vision. This was something else." He shook his head. "They tried to scare us. Killing me in the process. Or so they thought." He tapped his chest indicating his holy symbol on his character. "But she came to our aid and managed to slow the spell they put on me."

"What?" Lerissa stammered. "When did all of this happen?"

"Just now," Torinn answered. "We were taken from our meditation. They took us when we were at our most vulnerable. To threaten us, put fear in our hearts. As a way to sway us from our mission... our duty!"

"It was a bit more than a threat now wasn't it?" Ront said. "You did take a major hit."

"And I will be fine in due time, my friend." Torinn chuckled again, letting out another grunt of pain. "I just need some rest."

"Okay," Lerissa nodded. "Let's give you some privacy to rest. Please, no more getting murdered in your sleep."

"Yes, ma'am." Torinn smiled. "And carefully, with some help, I lay myself down to rest."

"And we leave him to do so," Lerissa added. "Outside his room, I want to chat with these two." She pointed at Ront and Rolen. "What the hell happened?" she whispered angrily.

"It was another one of those nightmares," Rolen answered.

"Obviously not." She gestured to Torinn. "This was not just a dream. Torinn almost died."

"I realize that," Rolen whispered back. "I don't know what you want from me. This is beyond my control."

"Hey, Matt," Lerissa turned towards Mr. R. "While they were off in the land of death, was I able to study at all about anything pertaining to our situation?"

"Give me an investigation check," he replied.

She rolled. "Twenty-seven."

"You managed to find some writings about a town in the middle of an invisible sea. Once a large international trading post between the continents, now a barren wasteland. The port city thrived as ships docked from every corner of the world. But one day the water disappeared. Nothing for miles. Just—gone," Mr. R portrayed.

"Was there anything in that city that piqued my interest?" Lerissa asked.

"There was mention of a warlock in the city. A being who has lived for thousands of years. Nobody has seen him since the water disappeared. They say that he's a myth. This warlock had been a keeper of knowledge for millennia. The second largest library in the western hemisphere. Just a few books short of the size of Dracomear," Mr. R explained.

"Maybe not anymore," Ront snickered.

"What about him has my attention?" Lerissa asked, ignoring Ront's remark.

"There was a brief section on a friendship he had in his younger years. One only referred to as The Master."

"He has ties to Death's Hand," Lerissa pieced together.

"So what does this mean?" Ront asked.

"That means he knows something," Lerissa answered. "He has inside knowledge."

"What makes you think that?" Rolen joined. "It's not enough detail to speculate that. What if they were friends before the dude became a genocidal maniac?"

"Did it say anything specific about their relationship?" Lerissa turned to Mr. R.

"The section you read wasn't really an account of the past, but more of a high alert watch page. A warning that this person may be a danger to Death's Hand. So they keep him on a close watch." Mr. R explained.

"Ugh," Lerissa groaned. "Still, if he's this important that they want to keep a close eye on him, he has to know something important," she speculated.

"So what do you suggest?" Rolen asked.

"I think we need to go and find him," Lerissa said.

"Are you sure about that?" Ront urged. "I'm just saying, we don't have a great track record when it comes to showing up at the doorstep of a powerful arcana user."

"This time's different," Lerissa pleaded.

"How?" Ront argued. "This time they didn't track us to a tavern. They waited for us and pulled us from your teleport spell. The only difference is that now they're aware of our movement."

"So what do you propose?" Lerissa folded her arms.

"I don't," Ront sighed. "I'm just saying we need to take precautions."

"So it's settled. We will make our way to the city in the morning," Lerissa stated. "And I head off to my room."

Ront eyed Rolen with concern. "I follow suit," Ront sighed.

"I guess I do too," Rolen shook his head.

"Alright," Mr. R nodded. "You all find your way to your room for the night. Some of you in a drunken stupor." He gestured to Gimble and me. "Others from near death trauma. But you all manage to rest the night away, regaining all used spell slots and damage."

EIGHT

THE CITY IN THE DESERT SEA

"You all wake and do your normal routines. Breakfast, study, sharpen weapons," Mr. R narrated. "Then coming to congregate in the front entrance before you head out."

"Are we ready?" Lerissa gauged the group. Everyone nodded silently. "Great, then let's get a move on."

"The party heads out the door, appearing again at the tree-line just before the cliff's edge, the sun beating down on you instantly. It is hot and miserable here, and it's still early in the morning."

"I change my mind," I said. "Let's go back to the mansion." I wiped my brow. I just got really hot thinking about it.

"We need to move," Lerissa instructed. "We need to move now, the longer we wait, the hotter it's going to get."

"Let's go then," Rolen repeated. "I take some cloth from my bag and wrap it around my head to protect myself from the sand."

"Smart," I said. "I angle my helmet forward and drape a cloth along the horns so I can see, but block the sand."

"You trek through the sand, occasionally readjusting your

protective clothing. Eventually, you get about a mile out, and begin to feel something sloshing on your feet." Mr. R paused.

"The longer you stand there, and the further you go, you begin to notice the moving sands burying your feet and the sloshing feeling moves further up your legs."

"Guys," I looked around. "What's going on here?"

"I'm not quite sure," Torinn responded. "It's as if... we're in water." He paused.

"What do you mean we're in water?" Ront asked.

"I'm not sure what I mean," Torinn shrugged. "But it's almost as if this isn't a desert at all. Didn't that book make note that the sea had just up and disappeared?"

"What are you getting at?" Gimble eyed his brother.

"What if the water wasn't destroyed. What if it was just hidden?" Torinn speculated. "What if we're standing in the midst of the sea that was once here?"

"I want to pitz a few notes and to cast see invisibility," Gimble said. "Do I see anything new?"

"You feel the arcane energy flow from the vibrations of your instrument and into your eyes. As a shimmer glosses across your eyes, and you all watch as his eyes begin to glimmer with a translucent purple to them. And Gimble, you look around and see a vast body of water that looks to spread for miles and miles. You look down to see that you are about waist deep in the water," Mr. R described.

"Well, I'll be! You were right Tor!" Gimble laughed, looking around at the floor in awe.

"So how do we plan on getting across to the city?" I asked concerned. "You know I don't do water."

"I cast walk on water for everyone," Rolen said.

Mr. R rolled behind his screen. "You all feel the familiar pushing feeling as you're lifted from the water and set on the surface. Each of you look like you're floating off the ground a few inches. The moving water like solid ground beneath your feet."

"Great, let's go!" I cheered. "And I take off towards the city."

"And like usual," Mr. R chuckled. "Adrik takes off towards the next stop. This time, he's followed by a very confused and eager owlbear."

"As we're walking, I want to talk to the rest of the gang," Lerissa said. "Any idea on how or why the water is invisible?"

"The obvious is that someone is hiding," Gimble speculated. "They cut off the world from this area. They're trying to keep people away from whatever is going on."

"Do you think it's them?" Lerissa asked.

"I wouldn't put it past them," Gimble agreed. "But they're in Seartia in the Southlands. Why would they cut off and destroy this city in the middle of the water?"

"It was a midway trading point," Rolen reminded. "They don't want any form of travel—someone accidentally stumbling upon whatever is going on there."

"So you think the city was just in the crossfire?" Torinn questioned.

"Sort of. They want to stop the world from coming to the area. At the same time, they have a person of interest supposedly living there. It's two birds with one stone. Cut the world off from them, and put him away from the world." Rolen explained.

"So he's a much bigger threat to them than we thought," Lerissa thought aloud. "We need to find this guy soon!"

"You guys walk along for the duration of the water walk spell, reaching the city just in time. You climb up a ladder to the dock, and when you pull yourself up onto the dock, you see a massive and empty city." Mr. R began to illustrate. He then tapped his keyboard and on the screen, a new image appeared.

This city was gigantic. Towers that stretched to the sky,

domes that seemed too large to be able to hold themselves up. It reminded me of ancient paintings of Constantinople; still gorgeous and stunning, but abandoned and desolate.

"You get a strange feeling as you look around and observe your new surroundings," Mr. R said. "Not quite sure what to make of this place. The elegant architecture... abandoned. No one to be seen anywhere. But a place of this magnitude, it just doesn't make sense to be empty."

"Hello?" I called out. "Is anyone home?"

"Adrik!" Lerissa whispered to me. "What are you doing?"

"What? It's empty!" I defended. "Nobody's here. Nothing is gonna happen."

Mr. R rolled his dice.

"We don't know if that's true," Ront said, slapping me upside the back of my head.

"Ow, what was that for?" I shouted.

"Shut up!" He whispered at me, now covering my mouth with his hand.

Mr. R rolled again.

"We're not alone," Gimble muttered. "Something's here."

"Roll me a perception check," Mr. R asked Gimble.

"Thirteen," Gimble replied.

"You do get that feeling that somethings here..." Mr. R rolled a third time. "And it's watching."

"Is my see invisibility still on?" Gimble asked.

"It would have worn off before you climbed the ladder," Mr. R said.

"Should I cast it again?" Gimble turned to Lerissa.

"What do you think it is?" She questioned.

"I'm not sure," he replied. "I just have this weird feeling. Like we're being watched."

"If you think it could do us good." Lerissa shrugged.

"I'm gonna pluck out the few more notes to cast see invisibility again," Gimble said.

"You feel your eyes adjust, like when you leave a dark area and go outside for the first time, the shimmering sparkle glinting over your vision. Once your eyes fully settle, you begin to notice the town is full of spectral beings," Mr. R described. "As if the whole town had died and become ghosts."

"What the..." He trailed off.

"You all begin to notice the owlbear—"

"Tordek," I interrupted.

"Tordek?" Mr. R confirmed with me. I gave him a quick nod. "You all notice Tordek wandering off curiously."

"Tordek," I called out. "Where are you going? And I follow."

"Ugh!" Ront groaned. "I tail him."

"You two begin to wander off behind Tordek as they take you up a back road," Mr. R narrated.

"Did I notice them wander away?" Rolen asked.

"Roll me a perception check," Mr. R told him.

"Twenty," Rolen rolled.

"You notice the two loudest in your group walk away followed by the large half-orc stalking behind," he described.

Rolen rolled his eyes. "I catch up with Ront."

"And what about you three?" Mr. R asked turning to the other half of the group.

"I wanna go straight up the first road right in front of me," Gimble said.

"I follow the man who can see," Lerissa announced.

"Ditto," Torinn agreed.

"Alright, let's start with the group following Tordek," Mr. R said, turning back towards us. "You guys follow the owlbear up and down some large main streets followed by small alleyways that Tordek has to squeeze through."

"Where are you taking us, Tor?" I asked.

"And just as you ask that, Tordek stops at a large wall in an alleyway and sits in front of it." Mr. R narrated.

"Where are we?" I whispered to Mr. R.

"Where the hell did your bear take us to?" Ront questioned me.

"It's a wall," I told him.

Mr. R clicked his keyboard, and the image on the screen changed to a painting of a brown owlbear looking up at tan stone wall.

"What does it want with the wall?" Rolen asked.

"What if," I pondered a moment. "What if I knock on the wall?" I knocked on the table.

Mr. R rolled a couple of times before speaking. "As you knock on the wall, you hear the knocking echo behind the wall."

"Ah-ha!" I shouted throwing my finger in the air!

"Ah-ha what?" Ront asked puzzled. "It echoed behind the wall. What's so special about that?"

"That means it's not just a wall, but a wall that's hiding something," I explained.

"Yeah," Rolen sighed. "It's a wall of a building. It's made to hide the insides. It's meant for privacy."

"You guys don't trust my instincts do you?" I asked sarcastically.

"What? No," Ront returned the sarcasm.

"I knock again." I knocked on the table again. Knock, knock... knock.

Mr. R rolled again. "As you complete your last knock on the wall, you are left there for a moment listening to it echo behind the wall. And once the echo falls silent..." He rolled again. "The wall begins to recede to the sides. Exposing a massive stairway that leads down."

"Ha!" I laughed at Ront. "Who's dumb now?" I leaned back and folded my arms.

"Never said you were dumb." He smiled. "Just not very bright sometimes."

"And with that comment, Tordek makes its way down the stairway." Mr. R directed.

"I follow again!" I exclaimed.

"Me too," Ront and Rolen said simultaneously.

"Okay," Mr. R nodded. "As you guys make your way down the stairway, I'm going to move to you three. We left you three as Gimble began walking into the city with you two in tow," he reminded.

"Is there anything I notice about all the people I see?" Gimble asked.

"Give me a perception check," Mr. R told him.

"Twenty-five," Gimble claimed.

"After observing the ghost-like figures, you get the feeling that they aren't just animate objects aimlessly floating around, but that they are all moving with purpose. Almost as if they are alive and unaware that the city is empty," Mr. R described.

"That's odd," Gimble muttered. "I'm seeing people. Like living people, living their daily life. But they're like ghosts; floating and transparent."

"What do you mean?" Lerissa asked.

"It's like they don't know they're invisible," Gimble tried explaining. "Life is just going on for them."

"Are they alive?" Torinn questioned.

"I'm not sure," Gimble replied. "Can I talk to them?" He asked Mr. R.

"You can try," Mr. R shrugged.

"Okay, I try and talk to the person in front of me," Gimble said. "Excuse me, pardon me."

"This woman who passes you, dragging her child by his arm

looks down at you but continues her path. Not paying you any more attention. The child, however, does try to play with you," Mr. R narrated.

"Okay, they can see us," Gimble laughed. "But they don't seem all too friendly about it."

"So is everyone just invisible?" Torinn asked.

"It seems that way," Gimble shrugged. "But why? I understand the water, but why the entire city?"

"Let's keep moving," Lerissa told them. "There has to be something here where we can get some answers."

"Well yeah," Torinn shook his head. "We're looking for some library that may or may not exist."

"As you utter those words," Mr. R began before rolling a handful of dice. "All three of you suddenly fall through the ground beneath you."

He clicked his keyboard again and the image changed from Tordek and the wall to a dark lair. The stones are a dark ashy gray. Torches adorn the walls but provide little to no light. Bright green moss seems to flood through the cracks and crevices of the stones.

"The three of you slam into a hard stone floor. Taking..." Mr. R trailed off and rolled. "Ten damage."

"Welp," Gimble smacked his lips. "I guess that answers that question."

"And coming down a staircase behind you three, a familiar looking owlbear." Mr. R narrated.

"Tell me it actually ate them and we're going to find their bodies on our way out," Lerissa joked.

"And behind Tordek you watch Adrik followed by Rolen and Ront come into view," Mr. R chuckled.

"Oh hey, guys!" I greeted them. "How did you beat us down here?"

"We fell from above," Torinn explained, pointing at the

ceiling.

"How did you find this place?" Lerissa interrogated.

"The bear led us," Rolen responded. A tinge of defeat in his voice.

"How did it find this place?" Lerissa asked.

Like robots, the three of us shrugged in unison.

"It just wandered over here. Like it knew where to go," Ront clarified. "But how?"

"Well it either has been here," Rolen started explaining. "Or something is drawing it here."

"But what?" Lerissa continued to ask.

"Well, our only way to find out..." Gimble pointed at the screen. "Is continuing forward."

"And you all turn to look down the hall that Gimble pointed to, and you see Tordek already making their way to whatever is beyond that hallway," Mr. R narrated.

"There's two of you now?" Lerissa groaned, staring at me.

"I don't hear that." I smiled. "I'm caught up to Tordek at this point."

"Good lord, there are two of them now!" She rolled her eyes.

"Well like you always say," Gimble laughed. "Better catch up with the dwarf before he gets himself killed."

"You all follow Adrik into the dimly lit hall?" Mr. R asked.

And like robots... they nodded.

"You all follow down a stone passage behind Adrik and Tordek. After what feels like forever and an endless passageway, you all come to a dead end. All six of you are collected in front of a stone wall; Tordek, nowhere to be found," Mr. R described.

"What happened to the bear?" Torinn asked.

"I don't know. I was following him when all of the sudden there was a wall in my way and Tordek was gone," I explained.

"For being a huge animal that's hard to miss, we seem to lose it a lot," Ront noted.

"Can I get a perception check from everyone?" Mr. R asked.

Lerissa let out a loud sigh. "Nine."

"Eleven," Rolen called out.

"Fourteen," Torinn nodded.

"Sixteen," Ront said.

"Fifteen," Gimble claimed.

"Sixteen," I finished.

"Alright, everyone but Lerissa hears a voice quietly echo through the passageway." Mr. R explained. "Did you bring them Gerbo? Did you find them?"

"What was that?" Ront asked.

"What was what?" Lerissa questioned.

"That voice," Torinn told her. "There's someone here."

"The voice begins to grow closer. But it sounds like it's coming from the wall in front of you." Mr. R illustrated. "Well, where are they?"

"I prepare my axe," I announced.

"Daggers," Ront stated.

"Well, what do you mean you left them behind the facade? You silly bear you," the voice chuckled. "And suddenly the wall before you disappears and in front of you stands a human man. He's tall and scrawny. Old-fashioned bifocal spectacles are carefully balanced on the edge of his nose, and a long white beard stretches from above his lip, down his chest, resting above his stomach. His thick head of silver hair is tied back away from his face. Baggy black robes hide his frail-looking body. Attached at his hip, a large black leather spell book in a large square holster dangles at his side. In his hand, he holds a tall wooden staff with a skull on top. The eyes of the skull glow a ruby red, and mist with arcane energy; something you all are very familiar with."

"Who are you?" Ront shouted.

"My dear child," the man grinned. "They call me Froug."

NINE
FROUG AND GERBO

"Is that supposed to mean something to us?" Ront interrogated.

Mr. R let out a low, ominous chuckle. A cheshire grin resting on his face. "I doubt it would." He chuckled again. "It rarely means much at this age. In fact, I don't think I've heard that name in many, many years."

"It's you?" Gimble asked. "You're the warlock we've been looking for! You are The Keeper of Knowledge!"

"That my friend, would be correct." Froug confirmed. "I am The Keeper of Knowledge. Master of all things written. I have a copy of every tome that was crafted. Every tale that was written. Every journal that was kept."

"So it exists?" Torinn blurted out. "The library, it's real?"

"As real as you or I," Froug nodded. "I brought you all here in hopes that you would find my resources any help at all."

"Brought us here?" Ront glared.

"Yes, brought you here." Froug repeated. "My old friend Gerbo here brought you to me. I had sent him out to find you all after I had heard word you were in Dracomear. And by the looks of it, he found more than we had hoped."

"Wait. You knew we were in Dracomear?" Ront pressed. "Did the whole world know we were in Dracomear?"

"Only those who have been looking," Froug chuckled.

"So why were you looking?" Lerissa asked.

"You six have made a lot of noise in my realm," he began. "I have been keeping an eye on you all since your little scuffle at the Dragon's Tale."

"That was our first run-in with Death's Hand," Lerissa mumbled. "You're one of them aren't you?"

"Oh, on the contrary my child." Froug shook his head, smiling. "I am one of you."

Everyone stared at Mr. R, puzzled. Unsure of what to say next.

"I know, that seems very unlikely. But believe me, I want nothing more than to see Death's Hand fall," Froug said, breaking the silence. "They have become erratic and dangerous. That was not the intentions we had when we started."

"So you are one of them!" Ront shouted. "I throw the Raven dagger at him!"

"Ront, no!" Rolen roared. But it was too late.

"As you throw your dagger towards Froug..." Mr. R began. "It freezes mid-air just inches away from his nose." Mr. R grinned again. "He moves his hand up and carefully pushes the dagger out of his face, the dagger floating away aimlessly in the air. He moves forward towards you," Mr. R said to Ront. "You are her champion... aren't you?"

"W—what?" Ront stuttered.

"I can sense her presence. It lingers behind you," Froug muttered. "But you don't resemble a champion of the Raven Queen. Your wings, where are they?"

"W—wings?" Ront struggled to let out. "I—I haven't had wings since she brought me back to life. What are you talking about?"

"All my life I have worked on the preservation of knowledge. I have met many champions of many pantheons. But there is something about champions of the sisters that separate them from any other champion," Froug rambled.

"What is it?" Torinn asked eagerly.

"That." He pointed at Torinn.

"Me?" Torinn looked at him confused.

"Your purpose. You are a champion of Pelor are you not?" Froug asked.

"Yes," Torinn replied. He looked even more confused. And I don't blame him.

"The sisters, Life, and Death, always play on balance. You can't have the one without the other. When one chooses a champion, the other one follows suit. Keeping the balance and order of the natural world," Froug explained.

"So what does any of this have to do with Death's Hand?" Lerissa interjected.

"Ah yes," Froug said. "Death's Hand is the opposite of the balance the sisters strive for. For years, no, millennia. Death's Hand has been terrorizing the world in the name of the Raven Queen for a long, long time. Everywhere they roam death follows. But through all the death they cause, they also cheat it."

"And that's where there is a lack of balance?" Gimble asked.

"Exactly." Froug nodded. "Long ago. Before it was called Death's Hand, I was one of the only two members. We had been researching and gathering as much knowledge as we could about the world we were in. We studied the arcane energy of the plane. The beginnings and growth of life. We studied the dying and the mechanics of passing to the next plane. But that's where we discovered everything... and where it all went wrong." He hung his head.

"What went wrong?" Ront continued interrogating.

"We stumbled upon a form of magic that granted magic

users the power to avoid death and prolong their life," Froug sighed. "That's where we became Death's Hand."

"I'm confused," Gimble interrupted. "You discovered immortality by accident, so you became a cult of genocide and murder?"

"Not intentionally." Mr. R's expression faded. "When we found what we had done, we immediately agreed that this magic should never be used for true immortality. Quickly after we discovered the process, word spread like wildfire. Arcane users of all incarnations began finding the key to longevity. We were summoned to the astral plane, home to your deities. They explained the balance and what a terrible mistake we have made destroying it. They charged us with a purpose, which slowly became our curse and downfall. We were to seek out those who have lived well past their expiration. And expire them ourselves."

"So you were told by the gods to kill people for your mistakes?" Lerissa asked.

"Yes. And in the beginning, it wasn't too bad. One or two beings every few years. But after a while, these magic users apprentices would have access to this knowledge. They would pass it down. After a while we were traveling the globe all day, taking life after life," Froug choked on his words. "That's where our views began to split."

"He wanted to make a point to those abusing the magic. Kill the innocent along with the abuser to show the world what happens when you abuse these dark magics," Rolen pieced together.

"Precisely!" Froug nodded. "Greg... you probably know him as The Master or The One. He began to grow a following. Beings from around the world began to realize how he had been able to outlive these powerful beings who had themselves lived longer than they should have. They found the key was to become close to him. Eventually, he began to realize his own mortality was no longer a thing. But what is worth living for, if you have nothing left in your life? Our charge became a dire curse."

"She sent you to end it?" Ront asked.

"And I had thought that I had." Froug took in a deep breath and let it out with a sigh of sorrow. "But that's what he needed to become what he is today. I created my worst nightmare. I created a powerful necromancer. One who is now immortal. And can avoid death, even after he has died."

"You created a Lich!" Torinn shouted.

"Not quite. He isn't undead. To be undead you must first fully die... and then stay dead. No, Greg has found a way to resurrect himself from beyond the grave. He is more powerful than I could've ever imagined."

"So what do Torinn and I have to do with this?" Ront asked.

"You are the champions of Life and Death themselves. Vestiges of divine powers beyond anything of this plane. Including Greg," Froug explained. "But you two are far from attuned to your arcane abilities. For heaven sakes, you don't have your wings." He pointed at Ront. "And you either." He turned and pointed at Torinn. "These are the first of many characteristics that the champions of the sisters possess."

"Well, how do we attune to these abilities—" Torinn began to ask before Ront interrupted.

"Are you serious Tor? You don't believe this crap do you?" Ront shouted.

"What do you mean? Of course, I do! You've had wings before. And we know that he is powerful. He nearly killed me from another part of the world!" Torinn defended.

"Yes, and if we take any longer to defeat him, he will become more powerful than we could fathom. And he's already beyond fathoming. We are out of time! I'm sorry, Froug. But we can't stay," Ront told his uncle. "Maybe if we survive this, we will come back and help you with whatever you need. But for now, we have family and a world that needs saving." He drew a deep breath. "Come on you guys. And I turn and head back up the stairs."

"It's the man isn't it?" Froug asked him. "And they don't know either, do they?"

"How did you—" He caught himself. "What are you talking about now, old man."

"They have your companion's granddaughters and son's wife. They have the druid's love. And they have..." He stopped. "You watch as the eyes of Froug's staff change from a ruby red to a darker blood red, the glow pulsing faintly."

"Say it! Tell them then!" Ront shouted. Tears welling in his eyes.

"He is your true love— isn't he?" Froug asked softly.

"Yeah, yeah he was!" Ront fought through the tears. "I thought I was protecting him by leaving. Nothing but a note as I abandoned him! Is this what you wanted to hear?" You could hear him fighting back the knot in his throat.

"I do not mean to hurt or offend," Froug consoled him. "But to defeat Death's Hand, you need to be open and honest with your companions. They took him, and now you need to save him."

"Was that who the other being was in our vision attack?" Rolen asked.

"Yeah," Ront sighed in defeat.

"Well, now we need to go," I spoke up. "There are more lives at stake now!"

"But you are not ready," Froug repeated.

"I don't think we can ever be ready," Ront shook his head. "He grows more powerful every second we spend stalling here! Now I'm going. Stay if you must... but I'm going—"

"Enough!" Gimble shouted. "Enough of this whole *I need to do this*, and *I need to do that*! We are a team, No! A family! That means your problems are mine and mine are yours! We stick together no matter what! Are you really willing to die alone? When you can live with your family?"

"He's right," Rolen joined. "What's the point of saving them if it's a suicide mission on your own? We are stronger together. But we will be more capable if we listen to Froug and build our abilities. We need to think through this logically."

"They have our loved ones!" Ront argued. "Are we willing to let them die so that we can train?"

"Are you really willing to let the entire world perish trying to save those lives? When we won't even manage to breach the front gates?" Torinn questioned.

"You have the most people in danger!" Ront reminded him.

"Which is why I'm thinking logically and not out of emotion. I have been planning on how to get them out of there since the moment I sent Kriv home," Torinn explained. "You realize we could have been to the Ruins already. We have two people who could teleport us there." He pointed to Gimble and Lerissa. "But if my plan is going to work, I need both of their teleport spells. For that to go well, we need to survive and then defeat him!"

"Then we need to get moving," Ront repeated. "If you want to beat him, then we need to attack sooner rather than later. Do you not understand what I'm saying?"

"Ront! You need to calm down and get some perspective on our situation," Torinn fought.

"You would rather them die than try to save them," Ront sighed. "I turn and walk back up the stairs—"

"I cast flame wall," Rolen interrupted. "I can't let you walk out on us. That's not how things work."

"Don't do this, Rolen," Ront growled. "Drop the wall and let me go. You don't want this to get ugly."

"It'll be ugly if you abandon your family," Rolen snarled back.

"We don't need to do this," Lerissa tried negotiating. "This will tear us apart just as bad if he walks out."

"So be it," Rolen said. "If he wants to split the party on his own selfish terms, then I'm going to try and unite the party on my own."

"So be it," Ront scowled. "I grip the Raven dagger tighter."

"I use my flaming fists," Rolen said.

"Enough!" Gimble shouted again. "I cast thunder wave! Everyone makes a constitution saving throw now!"

"Fifteen," I answered.

"Seven," Ront muttered.

"Twenty-one," Torinn called out.

"Ten," Rolen growled.

"Twenty-one," Lerissa announced.

"Great." Gimble shook his head and rolled. "Ront, Rolen, and Adrik are knocked back ten feet and take fifteen damage. Everyone else stays put but does take seven damage."

"You all hear Gimble shout and he pulls his bow across his strings. This deafening blast of energy blasts you all, sending you three backward and off your feet. The firewall drops and the roar echoes through the passage," Mr. R illustrated.

"You all need to get your heads out of your asses and listen to each other!" Gimble shouted. "If you keep on this petty, self-righteous loop, we're not going to get a chance to get stronger. They will wipe us out and we'll be sitting here picking our noses. So when you two are done acting like children, we need to have a real talk about saving the world. One that isn't driven by the emotion of a personal vendetta. At this point, we are soldiers on the front line! So get it together!"

We sat there for a couple of minutes trying to figure out what to say. Mr. R broke the silence.

"As you all try to gather a response, you all hear another ear-splitting boom, followed by a tremor. Bits of dirt and stone fall from the ceiling."

"What was that?" I asked.

"That, my friend," Froug frowned. "That is your cue."

"Well, stop standing around picking your nose," Ront said. "We're soldiers on the front lines!"

"I dart past him and head to the surface," Gimble narrated.

"I follow close behind," Ront announced.

"I presume everyone makes their way to the top?" Mr. R asked. We looked at each other for a moment.

"I do," I told him.

Lerissa and Torinn shrugged.

"Yeah, we go," Torinn answered.

"You're the only one left," Mr. R looked at Rolen.

He shook his head. "I..." He paused to think of what he was actually going to do. "I guess I follow them."

"Okay, you all make your way up the stairs, the bright sun blinding you all for a moment. You hear another boom echo through the city before the ground shakes again. This time you hear screams. And like a television getting bad reception, you watch as the entire population fades into sight for a brief moment before returning back to completely invisible again," Mr. R described.

"Which way did the boom come from?" I asked.

"Give me a perception check," Mr. R told me.

"Eleven?"

"You piece together that whatever this is, its epicenter is towards the town center," he explained.

"I head in that direction," I told him.

"We follow him," Lerissa said, looking around the table. Nobody argued against it. "Good, then we all go!"

"You all trek your way through the city, pushing through narrow alleyways, fighting past invisible crowds going the other way," Mr. R narrated.

"I grab Gimble, throw him onto my shoulders and take him up to higher ground with me," Ront directed.

"Okay," Mr. R nodded. "I need a strength check on Gimble and an acrobatics check on Ront."

"Nat twenty!" Ront cheered.

"Oh well, that makes mine even better." Gimble shook his head and laughed. "Natural one... with a minus one modifier on strength."

"Gimble, you feel a jerk as you're pulled off your feet and thrown onto Ront's muscular shoulders. You try to gain some form of grip, but just can't manage to get a hold of anything and you plummet back to the ground," Mr. R described. He started to roll his dice.

"Hold up," Gimble put his hand out to stop Mr. R from rolling more. "Before I hit the ground I'm going to cast dimension door. Specifically, I want to end up on the rooftops above Ront."

"Ront, you watch as your gnome friend falls from your shoulder and plummets to the ground. You wince as you anticipate the coming splat but you don't hear him hit the ground. You open your eyes and notice he's nowhere to be found. And your party is too far ahead to have caught him," Mr. R depicted.

"And you hear from above you," Gimble smiled. "Hey slowpoke, if you're done dropping people off buildings, we should get a move on!"

"How the—? What the—?" Ront mumbled to himself. "I hurry up the wall."

"As you make your way up the wall, and the rest of you head to the center of the city, you're hit with another boom, followed by a tremor. I need a constitution saving throw from all of you.

"Man, not again," Gimble sighed. "Eleven."

"Twelve," Ront groaned.

"Twenty-three," I called out.

"Nineteen," Rolen said.

"Thirteen," Torinn joined.

"Fifteen," Lerissa finished.

"Everyone but Adrik and Rolen are thrown off their feet," Mr. R began. "My rooftop boys, I need a dexterity saving throw from you both."

"Twenty-seven," Ront jumped.

"Twenty-three," Gimble cheered. They reached across the table and with a loud smack, they landed the greatest high five I've ever seen.

"You both slip as the building below you begins to give way to the tremors. You both go sliding off the side, but before you fall to your deaths... again," Mr. R chuckled looking at Gimble, who then promptly smiled back and gave him the finger. "You manage to catch the ledge of the building."

"This higher ground idea might be deadlier than I had hoped," Ront quipped.

"Let's hope it doesn't kill us, then," Gimble joked back.

"I'm gonna pull myself back up onto the roof," Ront said.

"The building is collapsing sideways. I'm just going to let you know, it isn't going to work, you'll slide right back off," Mr. R explained.

"Welp," Ront smacked his lips. "Can we manage to jump into the building we're falling towards?"

"You can try, for another acrobatics check," His uncle answered.

"Seventeen," Ront rolled.

"You manage to make the jump across the shrinking alleyway and barely make your way through a window on the next building over," Mr. R narrated.

"Twenty-four," Gimble called out. "I follow him through the window, landing in a glorious tuck and roll, rolling into a standing position and arms spread wide!"

"That you do." Mr. R laughed.

"I get back up and make my way up to the roof and continue back to the center," Ront described.

"Me too," Gimble agreed.

"Alright, to my other four," Mr. R said. "Two of you remain on your feet through the tremor. Lerissa and Torin, you both are knocked off your feet. All four of you give me a dexterity saving throw to avoid falling debris. The two who are prone, roll with disadvantage."

"Seventeen!" I blurted.

"Eleven..." Torinn said. "But I started with a seventeen." He looked at me and laughed.

"Natural twenty!" Rolen cheered, jumping up from his chair.

Lerissa dropped her head and shook it in shame. She held her hand up... index finger extended. "I rolled a nat twenty... and then my second roll was a two. So I ended up with a one."

"Alright," Mr. R chuckled. "Adrik and Rolen, you manage to escape unscathed. Torinn, you take three bludgeoning damage as a large chunk of stone clocks you on the side of the head. And Lerissa, you take ten bludgeoning damage as you're buried under large chunks of stone. You're pinned."

"Help me!" Lerissa cried out. "I can't get to my book!"

"I cast conjure minor elemental. I create a small earth elemental," Rolen said. "And I send it to help get her out from under there. I go and try to help."

"Give me a strength check with advantage for you and the

elemental," Mr. R asked.

"Fourteen for me. Nineteen for the elemental." Rolen answered.

"You both move towards Lerissa. With all your might, you both begin to lift and move rubble off her. I need a constitution saving throw from you." Mr. R pointed to Lerissa.

"Five." She cringed.

"As they remove the last bit of debris that had your leg pinned down, you're blasted with a huge shock of pain and the pressure that was keeping your leg in place is released. Your leg is mangled and definitely not how it should look," Mr. R depicted.

Lerissa grunted in pain. "Can I walk?" She mustered through the fake pain.

"No, your leg is too broken to even try to put pressure on it," Mr. R explained.

"I crawl my way over to her and cast cure wounds at second level," Torinn mustered. His voice weak to simulate the pain. "You regain nineteen hit points and your leg heals back up."

"You watch as Torinn crawls his way towards you, blood trickling from the side of his face. He lays a hand on your broken leg. His amulet begins to shine brightly. You begin to feel the bones and muscles in your leg move back into place. Small fragments of bone melding back with the larger sections. Your leg begins to look like it did no more than two minutes earlier," Mr. R illustrated.

"I get back onto my feet, help him off the ground, and continue our way to the city center," Lerissa described.

"As you all finally find your way to the center of the city, you emerge from a tight alleyway and come to the last building before a massive open area. In this colossal, circular, open space in the middle of a tightly packed city, you see a gigantic crater in the center, with cracks spreading across the remaining two-thirds of the original ground..." Mr. R paused. "Floating in the air above the crater, is a tall humanoid being in long, dark, flowing robes, with an Illithid mask obscuring the face. The being moves its decrepit and aged hand to the mask and removes it, and there behind the mask, the face of a young man presents itself to you. His right eye has been replaced with that of another being. The eye is glowing emerald green and the familiar arcane mist is billowing from the eye. A long scar that runs from the brow above the green eye, stretches down his face, over his lip, and deep past the collar of his robes."

Mr. R broke to take a drink from his glass. "You all suddenly get an ear-splitting screech inside your heads" He clicked his keyboard and an image of the creature before us appeared on the screen. "You hear the words echo in your head. I am the Master. I am the One. You will bend your knee in servitude willingly... or I shall bend it for you, before taking your life." Mr. R cleared his throat. "I need everyone to roll initiative."

TEN

THE GOOD, THE BAD, AND THE UNDYING

"Five," Lerissa groaned as she announced the first roll.

"Seven." Torinn rolled his eyes.

"What the heck? Eight," Rolen sighed.

"Thirteen," Gimble shrugged.

"Eleven." I frowned.

"Well..." Ront teased. "I got a twenty-two."

"Well alright, this will be exciting," Mr. R nodded side to side. "Greg will have the first move as an attack of opportunity. You watch as an evil smile stretches across his face. He raises his hand high above his head." He looked across the table, scanning us all, and stopping to look at each of us individually. "So be it," he snarled. "His hand begins to absorb arcane energy that seems to come out of nowhere, and coalesces, swirling in his hand. Once it grows to about the size of a basketball, he slams it down into the ground with a deafening boom! You all feel the earth beneath you shake once again. This time, the cracks that spread from the crater in the center begin to split open. I need a dexterity saving throw from my four on the ground."

"Eighteen," I called out.

"Fourteen," Torinn said.

"Fourteen as well," Rolen nodded.

"Eight." Lerissa hid her face in her hands.

"Beneath the four of you, the ground begins to split open," Mr. R explained. "Adrik, your natural instincts kick in and you dive away from the impending devastation of the fissure. However, the other three of you are not as quick, and you fall towards the bottom of the fissure. You each get a reaction while falling."

"I cast meld with stone," Torinn blurted out.

"You reach out as you're falling and get a graze of stone. You feel your hand get drawn into the wall of stone as you slowly morph into the wall," Mr. R described.

"Can I reach out for Lerissa?" Torinn asked.

"You only get the one action on reactions," Mr. R answered.

"Don't worry about her," Rolen said. "I cast polymorph on her. I want to turn her into a hawk."

"What are you doing?" Lerissa shouted at her brother.

"No time!" Rolen responded. "Are you willing to polymorph?"

"What are you doing?" Lerissa repeated.

"Are you willing to morph?" Rolen shouted.

She nodded. She was fighting back imminent tears. She knew what her brother was about to do for her.

"As you plummet towards the craggy ground below, Lerissa, you feel your body shift into a hawk. It takes a moment to adjust. But you manage to get your wings under control," Mr. R narrated. "You float yourself in the air. You have an action."

"I—I..." She choked out. "Can I dive bomb and grab him?"

"You can, but he's going to be way too heavy to carry," Mr. R told her.

"Can I at least slow his descent?" Lerissa asked.

"Give me a strength check on it," Mr. R said as he began

flipping through his manuals. "But it's a minus three on the roll."

"Nat twenty!" she cheered. "But it still comes out to a seventeen."

"You swoop down and bury your talons into Rolen's shoulders. Rolen, you do take," Mr. R rolled, "two points of piercing damage. But Lerissa manages to slow you down to where you don't splatter across the ground. You do both crash onto the ground, taking... ten falling damage. Lerissa, you lose your hawk form and take the additional nine damage."

"Are you alive?" Lerissa asked, panting for air.

"For now." Rolen laughed.

"Okay, let's get into the combat." Mr. R smiled. "Ront, you're first."

"How high off the ground is he?" Ront asked.

"From what you can tell he's ten to twelve feet in the air," Mr. R described.

Ront swished his cheeks back and forth. "Does he see us up top?"

Mr. R rolled. He chuckled. "He does not."

"Perfect, I'm going to take my bow and dag him in the chest with it," Ront smiled.

"In your current position, you're more facing his back than his chest," Mr. R explained.

"Then I send it through his back and out his chest," Ront corrected. "Twenty to hit?"

"Hits," Mr. R nodded.

"I need d6's!" He demanded. "I need seven d6's."

And without skipping a beat Daryl poured six, six-sided dice in front of Liam.

"Thanks," Liam said to Daryl. He scooped up the pile of dice, shook them in between his hands, and let them go. The seven individual dice flying across the table in different directions. He pulled them all back in and calculated in his head and on his fingers. He looked at his uncle with a frown of approval. "Twenty-eight damage!"

"As you peer over the edge of the rooftop and look down at the scene below you. Instinctually, you pull out your bow, nock an arrow, and carefully aim at Greg's left shoulder blade." Mr. R paused. "And like a scene from any movie where the main character is an archer, a moment of slow-motion overcomes you: the release of the arrow as you exhale, the feathers grazing across your cheek as it flies past. The arrow then soars through the air until it finds its mark. You hear him holler in pain as the arrow-head pierces into his back, through his heart, and stops just outside his chest."

"And for my bonus action I'm going to duck back behind the roof's edge," Liam explained.

Mr. R rolled. "He does not see you. Gimble, you're up."

Gimble turned to Ront. "Keep me covered."

Ront nodded.

"I cast mislead. I turn invisible and a duplicate of me appears where I was sitting. I'm going to move him a few rooftops over and get the attention of Greggy poo down there, and try to turn him away from us and keep your sneak attack damage," Gimble strategized.

"Alright, now the spell itself is an action. And to move the duplicate is also an action so the movement will have to wait until your next turn," Mr. R explained. "But you do disappear for a moment. And then reappear in the same spot."

"Perfect," Gimble said. "Then for a bonus action may I inspire Ront?"

"And how do you do so?" Mr. R asked.

"In the inspirational words of Joe Esposito in The Karate Kid... *You're the best! Around! No one's ever gonna keep you down! 'Cause you're the best! Around!"* Jake sang, bobbing his head and doing the cheesy reach and pull with his hands.

"Alright, Ront, you have one d10 inspiration that you can add to any attack or saving rolls," Mr. R explained. "Adrik, your turn."

"I would like to frenzy rage, and then I would like to use all three actions to hurl javelins at him," I told Mr. R.

"Give me some attack rolls." He nodded.

"Nineteen, twenty-four, and a nat twenty which becomes a twenty-nine total to hit," I announced my rolls.

"Go ahead and give me the damage," Mr. R blinked with surprise.

"Nine and five for the two that did not crit." I rolled again. "And sixteen on the final throw."

"As you watch Greg turn to find who left their arrow in his chest, you hurl the first javelin at him. It lands in his back just under Ront's arrow. He turns back towards you as you volley the next javelin, which finds its mark in his shoulder. As he finally turns to fully face you. You launch the third and final javelin. It lands in his chest opposite the arrow still protruding from his heart," Mr. R illustrated. "He is growing angrier with every hit."

"I want to finish my turn taunting him." I smiled. "Hey ugly, did you extend your life because you couldn't find anyone to love your fugly mug?"

"His green eye flares at you. Make me a wisdom saving throw," Mr. R directed.

"Is he trying to frighten me?" I questioned.

"Maybe," he replied coyly.

"Well, in my rage I'm immune to being frightened." I shrugged.

"Then never mind." Mr. R laughed. "Rolen, we're back to you."

"I want to use one of my wild shapes and turn into an adult red dragon," Rolen said.

"As you both lay at the bottom of the fissure, suddenly, Lerissa, you watch as Rolen's form begins to change dramatically. Red scales replacing his skin. Large claws replacing his hands. A snout growing from his nose. Where once Rolen laid on the hard ground, now sits a large, red dragon," Mr. R depicted.

"I bow my head down to allow her to climb onto my back," Rolen described.

"I climb up." Lerissa nodded.

"Once she's on I take off to the top again," Rolen said. "Stopping to get Torinn."

"Now I should let you know, this fissure is only ten feet wide. Your wingspan is also ten feet. So you won't be able to take off at the bottom. Although about half way up it opens a little wider. You just need to get up to there," Mr. R explained.

"I guess we're climbing." Rolen shrugged. "Hold on."

"I need a strength check on Lerissa," Mr. R asked.

Lerissa rolled. "Fourteen."

"Alright. As Rolen moves his way towards the cavern wall, you grip tight and place yourself against one of his back spikes, you hold yourself against the dragon as he climbs his way out of the fissure," Mr. R narrated. "Torinn, you're up."

"I can see him coming up the wall, correct?" Torinn asked.

Mr. R nodded.

"Then I'm going to drop stone meld and drop down on him," Torinn described.

"Wait, what?" Rolen asked, concerned.

"Alright, I need a perception and a dexterity check on your catching abilities. As well as an athletics check to see how close you've gotten to him," Mr. R told Rolen.

"You're senile," Rolen muttered.

"Only on Fridays." Daryl winked and shot his finger guns.

"So my perception is based on my regular stats, correct? While the physical stuff is off an adult red dragon?" Rolen asked Mr. R.

He nodded again to confirm.

Rolen took in a huge breath. "Fifteen on perception."

"You manage to see Torinn suddenly appear from the stone above and plummet towards you," Mr. R began.

"Eighteen, athletics."

"You've managed to make it quite a ways up the wall. Maybe twenty feet or so below him."

"And a fourteen on my dexterity..." Rolen winced.

Mr. R rolled. "You just barely..." He drew a breath and sighed. "Catch him." He broke his frown with a huge smile.

Rolen, who had held his breath on the catch, let out a big sigh of relief. "Oh thank the gods!"

"Onward mighty, Rolen!" Torinn cheered.

"Lerissa, you're up," Mr. R said, turning to Laura.

"I hold on tight and take the lift to the top of the fissure," Lerissa replied.

"Alright, now it's my turn," Mr. R grinned. "After taking some heavy damage from the small and rather annoying dwarf, Greg turns a hand to you, his fingertips beginning to glow brightly. As the energy builds in his hand, you hear his voice in your head again." Mr. R cleared his throat. "Fools! I will destroy you where you stand!"

"Good luck with that! If *I* haven't killed us yet, I don't think anything will!" I taunted.

"And with that banter, the energy in his hand blasts at you. I need you to make me a constitution saving throw," Mr. R said.

"Twenty-seven," I answered.

"Alright, you take twenty-one points of radiant damage,"

Mr. R rolled. "And that ends his turn. Back to the top of the round. Ront, you're up."

"I'm going to dag him with another arrow," Ront said. "Thirteen?" he winced.

"Hits," Mr. R nodded.

"Seriously? Isn't he supposed to be some super powerful arcana user?" Ront questioned. "Never mind. I don't want you to get any ideas. He takes thirty-seven piercing damage."

"And that's with sneak attack damage added?" Mr. R asked. Ront nodded.

"Okay. Again, you pop over the edge of the building you're camping out on. This time not as carefully aimed. You draw your bow and let it go. The arrow soars before planting itself in Greg's lower back," Mr. R illustrated. "He lets out a wail of pain as the arrow lands inside him. I need a wisdom saving throw from Ront, Gimble, and Adrik."

"Seventeen," Ront said.

Gimble rolled. "Thirteen."

"Fourteen." I frowned.

"Gimble and Adrik, you both take eight psychic damage. Ront you take four," Mr. R listed. "You all hear a high pitched screech, leaving a piercing pain in your head."

"What did I just trigger?" Ront mumbled.

"Is that your turn?" Mr. R asked Liam.

"Oh right," he remembered. "I duck back behind the wall."

"Alright, Gimble," Mr. R said turning to Jake. "I need a concentration check from you."

"Don't ask that from me," Gimble groaned. He rolled and looked up with a smug grin. "Nat twenty!" he cheered. "Take that Lich boy!"

"You manage to keep your duplicate." Mr. R nodded.

"Good, because I want to move him to the other side of the city center," Gimble explained.

"How fast can it move?" Mr. R asked.

"It has double my movement. So fifty feet," Gimble answered.

"Okay, it can make it almost to the other side from you. Just past halfway," Mr. R said.

"I wanna get him to start jumping and shouting at Greg," Gimble explained. "Hey, butt munch! Like the arrows in your back? You're welcome!"

"Greg spins to face the duplicate. His eye flashes green again. I would like a wisdom saving throw from you," Mr. R requested.

"You sure about that?" Gimble bantered. "How's a twenty-two sound?"

"You feel a small tickle in your head, but nothing becomes of it," Mr. R depicted. "Adrik, you're up."

"Europe?" I tried to joke. But it didn't stick. "I'm still in my frenzy rage so I will try to move on him with my axe." I rolled my three attacks. "Twenty-six, nineteen, and eighteen. "

Mr. R nodded. "All three land." I rolled some more. "Thirteen, seven, and nine."

"You go barreling at Greg, who is floating in the air. You swing once, twice, all three swings barely reaching the torn ends of his cloak. He is unaffected." Mr. R grinned.

"You're kidding me, right?" I protested. "Three high rolls to hit and they don't land? Not even the twenty-six?"

"Oh, they would have hit. However, you are barely four feet tall and he is ten feet in the air. The math just doesn't make it," Mr. R chuckled.

"Come on, I'm resourceful! I would have realized that and found a way to get myself higher up," I argued.

"Okay, I'll make you a deal. Roll me a perception check with disadvantage." Mr. R shot his index finger up. "If you succeed, I'll retcon it."

I glared at him, gave him the ol' Clint Eastwood stare down. I grabbed my d20 and moved my hand next to my hip as if I were about to draw a pistol. "Wabam!" I shouted as I threw my d20 across the table. It ricocheted off the lip of the table under Jake's arms and flew back towards me, finally coming to rest right beside my soda can. I twitched my eye at Mr. R before looking away to check my roll. It's a seventeen.

I grabbed the die again, locking my gaze back at Mr. R. Ben began to whistle the theme to The Good, the Bad, and the Ugly while Torinn did the wailing part. I glared across the table for dramatic effect. "Whapah!" I blurted out as I gave my die a large toss in the air.

It arced high up and landed right in the middle of my half a slice of pizza. I slid the plate to Ront. I was not about to break this intense stare down.

Ront leaned over and whispered in my ear. "Nineteen."

I shot out of my chair! "Yeah, I'm feeling lucky, Punk! Twenty-two total for my lowest roll! Take that Greg!" I mocked.

"Alright," Mr. R nodded while folding his arms and leaning back in his chair. "We rewind back to Adrik running at Greg. Instead of foolishly running beneath the floating menace, Adrik darts off to the right a little and climbs a decent-sized spire protruding from the shattered earth. He takes a leap off the end, axe held high over his head. And he slams Greg in the chest." Mr. R sat back up in his chair and rolled behind the screen. "The blow was strong enough for you to pull Greg out of the air and to the ground. Giving you the opportunity for you other two strikes. Dealing the total twenty-nine damage."

"That's right!" I growled.

"That moves down to the three in the fissure below," Mr. R said.

"Have we moved to a point where I can spread my wings?" Ben asked.

"Yes. You have climbed far enough to manage full wing-span," Mr. R responded.

"Then I do just that," Rolen smiled. "I suggest you two hold on!"

"I need a strength check from the two on your back," Mr. R requested.

"Sixteen," Torinn called out.

"Why is this happening to me tonight?" Laura whined. "Six."

"As the dragon blasts off the wall, Torinn, you hold tight. Wedging yourself in securely," Mr. R narrated. "But Lerissa isn't so lucky. The force of the rising dragon and gravity against you throws you from the dragon's back, sending you flying back down. Give me a dexterity saving throw with disadvantage to see if you can grab the tail."

"I seriously think this is broken. I rolled another six," Laura sighed.

Mr. R took a deep breath before chuckling. "And in a feeble attempt to grab hold to the dragon's tail—"

"I cast conjure celestial!" Torinn blurted out.

"Alright," Mr. R shrugged. "What happens?"

"I create a pegasus to swoop down and save her from falling," Torinn depicted.

"Okay. In a blinding flash of light, a white pegasus appears floating in the air," Mr. R narrated.

"Go save her!" Torinn shouted.

"And with that, the pegasus looks at the plummeting tiefling. It adjusts its float into a dive behind Lerissa," Mr. R continued. "Give me a strength check on the celestial."

"Seventeen?" Torinn squinted.

"And with a swoosh and a humph the pegasus catches Lerissa and begins flying to the surface. I need another strength check," Mr. R said turning to Laura.

"At this point, just start rolling my fall damage." Laura rolled her eyes. "Eleven."

"The pegasus jerks upward, throwing you to the side—" Mr. R paused. "But you manage to just hold onto the mane."

Lerissa let out a massive sigh. "Thought I was for sure done for."

"And with that, the three of you crest over the ledge of the fissure returning to the surface. Which comes to Greg's turn." Mr. R scanned his notes. "Okay, he removes Adrik off his chest and floats back into the air. Anger swelling in his eyes," he depicted. A menacing smile across his face. "You fools dare defy a god?" He bellowed. "And with those words, he raises a hand to the sky. Dark clouds fill the once clear blue sky, swirling above the city center. As the three of you make it to the surface, a bolt of lightning strikes Greg's hand in the air, the electricity traveling down his arm and across his chest You can see a few sparks across his eyes. He aims his other hand at Adrik and blasts an arc of lightning at him. I need a dexterity saving throw from you." He gestured to me.

I craned my head and cracked my neck, scooped up my d20 and gave it yet another roll. I looked down at my die and almost screamed. "Three!" I shouted. "That only makes five," I let out with a defeated sigh.

"As the lightning strikes your chest, you take sixty-one points of lightning damage., Mr. R said.

As I went to subtract the damage from my current hit points. A sentence caught my eye on my sheet.

You gain advantage on dexterity saves against visible attacks.

"Hold on!" I blurted out. "I have advantage if I could see the attack. I had to have seen that attack!"

Mr. R furrowed his brow in thought for a second before he spoke. "I'll allow it."

I grabbed my die and gave it a light toss in the air. "Sixteen?" I asked.

"Sadly, that doesn't make it still. You still take the sixty-one points of damage," Mr. R explained.

"Surely you can't be serious!" I argued.

"Yes, I'm serious," Mr. R assured me. "But please, don't call me Shirley," he recited from one of his favorite movies, *Airplane*.

Liam let out an annoyed groan.

"Anyways. I need a dexterity saving throw from my three returning from the fissure," Mr. R continued.

"Wait, why?" Laura questioned.

"The mechanics of the spell," Mr. R answered her.

"Good god." Torinn sighed. "Seventeen."

"Nat twenty!" Rolen cheered.

"Ugh!" Lerissa growled out. "One."

"Natural one?" Mr. R asked her.

"No, it was a two," Lerissa groaned.

"Alright, Lerissa and Torinn also take sixty-one points of lightning damage. Rolen, you take thirty points of damage to your dragon form," Mr. R dished out. "This bolt of lightning that you all watched blast Adrik in the chest now shoots from his back and hits all three of you. All four of you feel your muscles tense and lock up. Your jaws slam shut to the point your teeth feel like they might shatter. Your eyes roll back into your skull. The intense moment of pain feels like it lasts forever... but the moment passes. The three in their normal forms come out with smoke and crazy afro-like hair, with residual static still sparking through your hair. We move back to the top of the round. Liam, your turn."

ELEVEN

BROTHERS OF ANOTHER LIFE

"I'm going to pop back over the ledge and give our pal another little gift," Ront explained. "Eleven?"

"Hits," Mr. R said.

"Just a casual thirty-five piercing damage," Ront smirked. "And I dive back behind cover."

"As another arrow finds its mark inside the back of Greg, he spins around to see the attacker, whom he presumes would be the galivanting gnome running along rooftops. You all watch as he flies higher up, moving towards the gnome. Gimble, your move," Mr. R directed.

"I take the duplicate and run him away from myself and Ront," Gimble explained. "And then I want him to jump into a barrel like a rodeo clown."

"With little to no effort, the duplicate Gimble hops, runs, and dives across the rooftops before leaping into a random barrel on the roof," Mr. R described.

"Wow, I didn't actually think that was going to work." Gimble laughed.

"Adrik, it's back to you," Mr. R said turning to me.

My eyes grew wide and my frown stretched across my face

as I stared at my sheet. I had no idea what to do. I can't attack him anymore from a distance. He's got my javelins in his chest still. I don't have any other ranger weapons really. But maybe this will work. "I want to take out both my hand axes. And then I'm going to huck them at sparkly eye in the sky." I rolled. "Nineteen and twenty."

"Both hit. Is that twenty a crit?" Mr. R asked.

"No, non-natural," I answered.

"Okay, roll some damage."

"Eight for the first axe. And ten on the second," I told him.

"And with all your might, you throw both these axes at Greg, both landing into his back. Each hit knocks him off to the side and down a little. But he moves and corrects himself, turning back to you," Mr. R continued.

"And with that, I run back to the dragon riding a dragon." I laughed.

"That moves us to Rolen," Mr. R said.

"First I bow my head to let Adrik onto my back," Rolen began. "And then once he's on I launch into the air over Greg and with a big smile, I'd like to blast him with fire!"

Mr. R blinked with surprise. "O—okay." Mr. R began frantically sifting through his notes and papers. He rolled a couple dice. Read a little bit. Then rolled a couple more times. "You all watch as the massive red dragon flies towards Greg. It halts over him, inhaling a long deep breath. And as the smile on the dragon's face grows, you watch as his stomach begins to glow. The light travels up the dragon's belly and its throat, and from his mouth, a blast of fire spews out!" Mr. R depicted. "Greg's once prominent form is now swallowed by flames. The buildings behind vanish in the blinding light, with smoke pluming from the burning area. Once the fire stops, nothing is left but soot and ash."

"Is that it?" I asked.

"It can't be?" Lerissa mumbled. "He was supposed to be a high mighty power to defeat."

"As you all question what just happened, Froug comes hobbling into the square with Gerbo behind him," Mr. R explained. "My Friends," Froug grunted. "W—what happened?"

"Well—" Torinn shrugged. "Your old pal Greg made a surprise appearance. He was what all that rumbling was."

"Yes, I knew that," Froug said waving his hand in the air as if to shoo the explanation away. "I mean what happened to him?"

"We killed him," I explained.

"You did?" Froug questioned. His eyebrow arched high.

"I'm going to come down from the rooftops," Ront said. "Yeah, we killed him. Thanks to our powerful druid friend up there." He gave Ben a friendly punch.

"I drop wild shape back to my normal self," Rolen described. "I just blasted him into oblivion."

Mr. R rolled some more dice.

"I feel like that was too easy," Lerissa continued to question.

"I—I think you may be correct," Froug stuttered. "Froug raises his hand and points behind you all. His curved finger visibly shaking. When you all turn to see what he's pointing at, you see a vortex of swirling black shadows. Dirt and sand are being thrown around. You all move to protect your faces, and when it dies down, you all move your hands to see again. There, floating in his previous spot, stands Greg once again." An evil smile crept across his face. "Did I not mention that I truly am a god? You think killing me was going to be that easy? Pathetic mortals. Welcome to your doom!"

"I loose another arrow at him," Ront blurted out. "Twenty-nine."

"You send this arrow flying like before. This one on course

for his skull. It lands between his eyes. He stares at the arrow now protruding from his face and gives his menacing smile again," Mr. R began. "You mortals are beginning to grow on my nerves." Greg growled. "He reaches up and pulls the arrow from his skull. When you anticipate blood pouring out, all you see is this nasty green pus that forms into the hole, closing the wound."

"This can't be happening," I muttered.

"What?" Greg snarled. "You don't believe what's before you? What you see with your very own eyes?"

"How?" Ront asked.

"Isn't it obvious child?" Mr. R's grin began to curl like a Dr. Seuss character. "I am beyond the magic of this plane! I have become a god! I have defeated nature itself! There is nothing that will stand in my way!"

"I raise my amulet into the air and cast divine word against Greg," Torinn said.

Mr. R flipped through his handbook. Scanning through page after page until his hand stopped. I presume on the spell he was looking for. He rolled some dice before looking to Torinn. "What's your spell DC?"

"Seventeen," Torinn answered.

"Alright," Mr. R nodded. "You all watch as Torinn raises his amulet high above his head. You all hear him whisper something under his breath. His amulet glows bright white. The light blasts out blinding all of you for a solid minute. Once all of your vision comes back, you all look around and see that Greg is nowhere to be found once again. And neither is Froug."

"Where's Gerbo?" I asked, concerned.

"He's looking around for Froug. But can't seem to get a trace on him," Mr. R explained.

"Where did they go?" Ront questioned. "They can't just up and disappear. What did you cast?" He turned to Torinn.

"Divine word. His hit points must have been low enough that he either died again or was banished from our plane." Torinn explained.

"Then what about Froug?" Gimble continued the investigation.

"That I don't know about," Torinn shrugged.

"So now what?" Ront wondered. "What do we do now?"

"We still have to save those he took from us," Rolen answered. "We still need to go south."

"What about this city?" Lerissa challenged.

"What about it?" Torinn tipped his head.

"There are people here, that are now forever stuck in an invisibility spell. And on top of that, their city kind of got a bit destroyed," she reminded us.

"They didn't seem to have a problem with the invisibility before, why should we change that now?" Ront asked. "We—"

"We need to focus on the task at hand," Torinn interrupted. "Froug is missing after we killed this so-called god for a second time. There are also innocent lives still to be saved and protected."

"How are we going to find Froug?" Lerissa questioned.

"I can try to scry on him," Rolen piped up. "If he's on our plane at all I can try to find him."

"So are you casting scry?" Mr. R confirmed with him.

"Yeah." Rolen nodded. "I walk over to Gerbo and sit in front of him. I reach out to use Gerbo as an artifact to find him. And then I close my eyes and focus on Froug. He needs to make a wisdom saving throw against my eighteen spell DC."

Mr. R nodded and proceeded to roll his dice. "You sit there for a moment. You focus your energy out to the arcane field that surrounds the world, searching for a familiar energy," He started to describe. "Gerbo acting almost as a satellite amplifying your energies. You sense his presence, and like a bird taking to the sky you feel a rush of air as you mentally rise off the ground before zooming towards the earth far away from your origin." He paused to click his keyboard. "And you come into a stone spire, high in the air with green arcane energy lighting the design in the floor. In the center of the flat top of the spire, a small obelisk balances a black bowl-like object on its tip. In the bowl, a swirling mass of blue and white arcane energies chase each other like koi fish in a pond." He pointed at the image on the screen.

"On the far side of the spire floor, is a small child. A gnome child is chained between two parts of the continuing spire. You spin around, and there, chained between two more pieces of the spire, is Froug, beaten and bloody. Finally floating out of the spire is Greg. From what you can tell he's giving a grand speech to what looks like an army of thousands. He turns back towards the bowl and obelisk and behind him, two kobolds drag a young woman against her will onto the spire."

"No!" Rolen shouted.

"And with that," Mr. R continued. "You are pulled with extreme force and thrown back into your body. Still sitting on the forest floor in front of Gerbo."

"Th—they have them! All of them!" Rolen stammered. "Elfi, Froug, random children... and an army!"

"An army?" I questioned him. "What do you mean, an army?"

"What the hell do you think I mean when I say Greg has a freakin' army?" Rolen snapped. "There were thousands of them! Cheering for whatever was about to go down! We need to hurry there!"

"How are we getting there?" Torinn asked.

"I'm sorry Tor," Rolen reached his hand out and placed it on Torinn's shoulder. "We need to use one of our teleport spells. We're out of time."

Torinn craned his neck. You could see his head move as his neck popped. He closed his eyes and let out a deep breath. "Alright." He sighed. "Let's do this!"

We all gathered our hands together and Lerissa began giving a pep-talk.

"This is it, you guys. We are low on health and spells—"

"I cast mass cure wounds on the group," Torinn interrupted. Torinn rolled a handful of dice. "Everyone gains thirty-one hit points back."

"Thanks." Lerissa smiled at him. "I definitely needed that."

Torinn nodded at her, acknowledging her thanks.

"Anyway," Lerissa continued. "We are low on spells, we are worn down, and we're a bit tired. But whoever said saving the world was going to be easy?" She looked over towards me, her smile widening. I could feel my face growing warmer. Even with the creepy red and yellow contacts lenses she still could make me melt. "We will now go blindly into the dark! Today is our independence day!" she recited.

I couldn't tell you anything more about that speech. She lost me in that smile, but it must have been a good speech, because everyone else was amped. They were all smiling with Lerissa and very engaged all of a sudden. So naturally, I went along with it.

"Let's do this!" Gimble cheered. "I cast teleport."

"And with that, you all can add 1d6 of inspiration from that riveting speech," Mr. R started. "As the inspiration settles in you, that feeling of confidence in your chest. You all feel the familiar rushing sensation of teleportation. The city around you begins to stretch as you're thrown across the world." Mr. R rolled a die. "And you guys appear in the ruins—at the back of the mass army."

"I cast invisibility at sixth level." Gimble jumped. "Hiding us all from the army."

"Close one," Rolen whispered. He shot a quick thumbs up before throwing his hand back in his lap.

"As you whisper that, a large orc turns around with a grunt." Mr. R said. He shifted his posture, hunching his back. His jaw moved from its normal position to a jutted underbite. He began sniffing and huffing around, like he's searching for us. "He scans the area around you all. Rolen, Lerissa, Torinn, and Ront each get a blast of hot breath in the face. Humid and putrid smelling, you feel the urge to hurl. But all manage to hold it down for the moment."

"I pull up my scarf to block the smell," Ront described.

"As you do so—" Mr. R rolled. "He moves his search to where you stand, Ront."

"I step back with my arms out to move everyone," Ront responded.

Mr. R sniffed around again. "I recognize that smell." He growls from deep in his chest. "I smell an abomination!"

"I quietly ready the Raven Dagger," Ront whispered. "Can I manage to move to the back side of him?"

"You can. Give me a stealth check with advantage," Mr. R nodded.

"Twenty-two and twenty-three," Ront announced.

"You slowly step around the orc, managing to get on his back side." Mr. R rolled again. He sniffed the air again before speaking. "And he slowly follows your scent and turns around. I will note that you are now in a massive crowd."

"That's perfect," Ront grinned.

"What are you doing?" Rolen whispered.

"Get to the spire. I've got you a distraction to get everyone out of there." Ront muttered.

"You need backup," Torinn argued. "I follow with him."

"What're you doing?" Ront hissed.

"There are thousands of creatures here." Torinn fought

back. "There's no way you alone can manage a surprise in the middle of an army and make it out. I'm coming with you! Besides, it's my duty to destroy them alongside you, isn't it?"

"And at this point, the orc is spinning in circles trying to figure out where these whispered voices are coming from." Mr. R chuckled. "I smell you, half human filth!" The orc growled. "I will find you!"

"You guys go!" Torinn ordered the rest of us. "We haven't much time!"

"My disciples," Mr. R broke out in a loud booming voice. "Servants of Death's Hand! Today we shall break the chains placed on us by the gods!" He raised his arms above his head. "Today we become—immortal!" Greg bellowed. "And suddenly the entire army begins to hoot and holler. Slamming their swords against their shields and fists against chests and armor," Mr. R described.

"Go now!" Ront shouted.

"I grab Adrik and Rolen by the arms and take off to the left flank of the army!" Lerissa called out.

"I follow behind her," Gimble directed.

"Alright," Mr. R nodded. He rolled some more dice. "You four hoof it around the massive army. Being quite some distance, you all make it to the left side of the cheering army when you hear Greg's voice boom over the audience again." he sipped his drink. "Tonight, we shall bring an end to the tyranny of those who hide in other planes. No longer will we just be known as man. No longer will we be the bottom of the pyramid. From this day forth, we will we the rulers of this world! And we will rebuild it in our own, new image! But first, my faithful servants, we must burn this world to the ground. So that it may rise up from the ashes and we will rule in our new glory! Today marks the beginning—" he paused. "Of the new world order!"

"We need to hurry up there!" Rolen said.

"Oh thanks," Lerissa shot back sarcastically. "I was really enjoying watching the new regime begin their preparations for global destruction!"

"I ignore her snarky comment and use my last wild shape to change into the adult red dragon once again," Rolen described.

"The three of you watch as Rolen becomes fully visible to you and then all of a sudden a large red dragon appears where he stood." Mr. R narrated. "And the entire army shifts towards the dragon—and begin charging at you!"

"Quickly get on his back!" Gimble called out.

"I help them both up onto the dragon before climbing up myself," I said.

"Once they get up on my back I'm going to fire blast at the charging army and fly up to the spire!" Rolen explained.

"As the remaining members of your party mount your back, you deeply inhale, your chest beginning to glow. With a massive blast, you release a fiery inferno from your mouth," Mr. R depicted. "War cries quickly evolve into screams of pain, and when the fire blast dies out, there is a giant, smoldering hole in the middle of the now awestruck army. Quickly they shake off their fear and begin charging again."

"Gotta blast!" Rolen blurted. "And I take off towards the spire."

"Alright," Mr. R nodded. "Ront and Torinn, are you going to remain invisible?"

"Yes—" Ront started before Torinn cut him off.

"I want to look for their ammunition and such. Something explosive!"

"Give me an investigation check," Mr. R cringed as he processed the request.

"Ten." Torinn winced.

"You search around looking for something. But in the commotion, you cannot find anything. And after being pushed and shoved enough you lose your invisibility," Mr. R narrated.

"Tor!" Ront shouted. "What are you doing?"

"Distracting?" Torinn shrugged.

"I guess I take the hit and start distracting too." Ront sighed.

"Alright," Mr. R chuckled. "You both get pushed around and drop invisibility. You two are now in the midst of this army of orcs, kobolds, and grungy-looking humanoids and halflings. You both stick out like two sore thumbs."

"I want to cast hallow around us," Torinn said. "And I want to use the fear component as well."

"Torinn, you bend down and touch the ground beneath you, your medallion glowing brightly. As an arcane energy seeps into the ground, a faint light illuminates the stone and grass around you. And as the ground takes the spell, you watch as some creatures can't pass the threshold. And those that do begin screaming and swinging their weapons as if to attack something that's not there," Mr. R described.

"That should buy us a little time," Torinn laughed.

"Let's hope it'll buy us enough time," Ront replied sarcastically.

"Alright, to my group with the dragon. You all go riding up to the spire. Once you reach it—" Mr. R rolled. "A blast of arcane power is thrown at you all. I need a dexterity check from Rolen. Followed by some strength saves from the rest of you."

"Nat twenty!" Rolen cheered, throwing his fist in the air.

"And the saving throws?" Mr. R asked.

"Twenty-one," I said.

"Sixteen," Lerissa asserted.

"Sixteen also!" Gimble smiled.

"As the arcane blast barrels towards you all, Rolen jerks upwards and away from the attack. Narrowly avoiding getting hit," Mr. R narrated.

"I swoop back around to get them as close as I can to the platform," Rolen directed.

"How close can we get?" I asked.

"You can get within feet of the platform without landing if that's what you're asking," Mr. R explained.

"Perfect!" I smiled. "Rolen, I need you to get us close to the platform."

"What's the plan here?" Lerissa glared at me.

"You guys swoop right above the spire. Rolen's wing just inches from the platform," Mr. R interrupted.

"Jump!" I shouted.

"Geronimo!" Gimble cheered.

"Oh good lord!" Lerissa groaned dragging her hand across her face. "I guess I jump!"

"The three of you jump onto the dragon's wing and slide towards the end of it. I need an acrobatics check from you three," Mr. R continued.

"Twenty-seven," Gimble said smugly. He leaned back in his chair folding his arms.

"Five." I winced. This is going to be my downfall, isn't it?

"Twelve?" Lerissa's squeaked.

"All three of you slide off the end of the wing. Gimble landing with a graceful roll, ending in the standing position," Mr. R started.

Gimble threw out his arms out wide a sang, "Look at me! I've come to foil your plans!"

"Lerissa, not quite as graceful, you land hard on your feet."

She dropped her face into her palm and shook her head.

"And Adrik—face first into the stone spire." He rolled. "Taking five falling damage."

I slammed my face onto the table and threw my thumb up over my head. "I'm good," I mumbled into the table.

"Ah good, the main event can begin," Greg hissed. "You

fools have brought me the last piece of the puzzle." He smiled and gazed at Lerissa. "Make me— a wisdom save."

"Fifteen," Lerissa called out.

Mr. R's smile grew wider. "You suddenly feel your body seize up. Like ice spreading across water from your toes to your face. You go to move, but your body doesn't cooperate"

"I cast counterspell!" Gimble interjected. "If that spell is lower than third level it's now failed!"

Mr. R stuck his tongue out in thought before nodding. "So to retcon that: you feel your body begin to tense and lock up, unable to move. You hear Gimble pull his bow across his strings, and feeling of warmth comes over you and you feel the paralysis begin to fade away."

"Nobody takes her from us! Not Reita, not death, and definitely not some green-eyed loser!" I taunted.

"Then it shall be your demise!" Greg hissed. "Brother," he changed his tone. It was frail and broken. "Don't do this Greg! I beg of you, don't do this!"

"Brother?" Rolen whispered to himself.

"Silence!" Greg boomed. "You are not my brother anymore, foolish old man!"

"What is happening?" I leaned over and asked Ront.

"Then why am I chained here? I know the ritual! I know the specific sacrifices you must make!" Froug pleaded. "One young and one old. Blood relation in between."

"They are related!" Torinn pieced together.

"Enough of this!" Greg shouted. "The ritual must commence!"

"I cast feeble mind!" Lerissa blurted out.

"Roll initiative," Mr. R replied.

TWELVE

SING THEE TO THY REST

"MAKE ME AN INTELLIGENCE SAVE," LERISSA ARGUED.

"What's the DC?" Mr. R asked.

"Eighteen," Lerissa glared.

Mr. R's shoulders dropped in defeat. "It's a fail."

"Drop his intelligence and charisma to one!" Lerissa cheered. "Want us to roll initiative now?"

"Yes," Mr. R smiled.

"But he can't fight," I argued. "He's dumber than I am!"

Mr. R rolled some dice. "From the swirling blue energy on the obelisk, a blast sends out a massive shockwave. You three make me both a strength saving throw as well as a wisdom saving throw."

"It's never that easy huh?" Gimble chuckled. "Nat twenty on my strength. But that's also a minus one so, nineteen. Eleven on my wisdom."

"Seventeen strength. Twenty wisdom," Lerissa listed.

"Twenty-one strength. Ten wisdom," I said.

He wrote something down on his scratch pad before looking back to us. "Rolen, everyone else is in some form of battle or combat. Before I move back to them. Is there anything you wish to do?"

"I want to circle and swoop." Rolen shrugged. "Fire blast a line of soldiers here, glaive a pocket of them there, scoop a battalion or two in my mouth and drop them on other battalions."

"Okay." Mr. R scrunched his nose.

That's usually a tell-tale sign that we've stepped past what he had planned. He had a whole thing planned for us here and somewhere we either ruined that or were more cunning than he anticipated.

"Alright." He clicked his tongue in thought. "Okay, you three." He pointed at Gimble, Lerissa, and I. "The shockwave pushes you back a little, but doesn't take you off your feet. However, Lerissa and Adrik, you both are going to take twenty points of psychic damage."

"We should probably deal with that," I commented.

"We also need to deal with him," Lerissa said pointing at Mr. R. "Adrik, you take on peanuts-for-brains. Gimble, you're on rescue duty. I'm going to figure out this bowl thingy."

"Aye!" I growled. "Frostbeard!" I shouted, my hands raised above my head.

"Roll me your attack," Mr. R said.

"May I rage?" I asked.

"Why not." Mr. R shrugged.

"Wonderful, because it's a twenty." I smiled. "And I'll take two swings." I rolled again. "Twenty-nine. I believe that hits as well." And before he could respond to my cocky response I rolled my damage. "Ten and twelve damage."

"You charge at the feeble-minded Greg, aimlessly floating in place. You land a bone-crunching slash into his midsection," Mr. R began. "Swinging the axe back around and landing it deep into his left shoulder. The powerful necromancer begins to wrinkle and age with every hit you make."

"Well, that's a good sign, right?" I asked.

"Gimble," Mr. R said turning to him.

"Well I'm going to start with Froug," Gimble answered.

"You run to the frail old man, dried blood trails down his face. He looks to you, his once vibrant eyes now glossed over and gray," Mr. R explained.

"Froug, are you alright?" Gimble asked.

"H—he is too strong! It's not going to work," Froug struggled to let out.

"Let's not worry about that right now," Gimble said. "Let's get you down from here."

"Gimble," Froug coughed. "Gimble, where are the angels? The half-orc and dragonborn?"

"They're a bit busy fighting the army down there," Gimble answered.

"T—take me to them," Froug requested.

"Are you strong enough to transport with me?" Gimble questioned.

"Strong enough," Froug mumbled.

"Then I use dimension door and take him to Ront and Torinn," Gimble shrugged.

"With a quick blink of your eyes, you and Froug suddenly appear in the middle of the battlefield. I need you to make a wisdom throw," Mr. R narrated.

"Five," Gimble winced as the word left his lips.

"As you open your eyes, you see your greatest nightmare. There is no longer an army charging. You are back home: Trick-leriver. The usually lush fields and sparkling river are now black," Mr. R described. "The little huts and homes you remember so well.; all ablaze. Screaming echoes in your head, and when you look back down at the ground, bodies litter the ashy floor. Some burnt, some mutilated, some unrecognizable."

"No," Gimble whispered.

"The screams begin to change into words. You did this! You killed us!" Mr. R hissed.

"No this can't be!" Gimble shouted. "I blink again and tele- port back to the spire."

"And with a blink, you're back where you last stood. No Froug and with a lack of breath," Mr. R narrated.

"I look out into the battlefield where Torinn and Ront are," Gimble panted.

"You see the two of them in the middle of a clearing. Soldiers rushing at them, but none seem to get much closer than the twenty-foot circle around them. Between them, Froug lies on the ground. And circling in the air, Rolen in his dragon form swoops in and out picking up and dropping soldiers. Blasting them with fire every so often," Mr. R explained.

"Then I move on to save Elfi," Gimble sighed in relief.

"Alright." Mr. R nodded. "Torinn and Ront, you hear a whoosh of arcane energy behind you both. When you turn around, you see a frail Froug and a panicked Gimble at your feet. And before you can say anything. Gimble bamfs out."

"Froug?" Torinn blurted.

"Cleric," Froug struggled to get out. "Rogue."

"Yes, we're here," Ront assured. "We're here!"

"I—I," Froug stuttered.

"Anything, what is it?" Torinn jumped.

"You must..." Froug coughed. "I need you both." He wheezed in taking a breath. "To kill me."

"W—what?" Torinn eyed Mr. R. "W—we can't! We still need you here!"

"You must—bring balance to everything!" Froug coughed again. "He can't become the undying god he wishes to be without me. The ritual requires a sacrifice of family both young and old."

"But that child up there is a gnome," Torinn reminded him.

"And so were we once," Froug muttered. "You have a lot to learn about true resurrection young champions."

"I pull out the Raven Dagger," Ront sighed. "Are you sure there is no other way?"

"I—I'm afraid not," Froug forced out.

"No!" Torinn argued. "We can find another way! There has to be another way!"

"My child," Froug whispered reaching out for Torinn and Ront's hands. "All life must come to an end. I have stayed well beyond my welcome. It is time for my soul to move on. It's time for me to return home—"

"I bury the dagger into his side," Ront interrupted.

"Thank—you," Froug muttered. A painful smile across his face.

"What have you done?" Torinn shouted.

"I did what was asked," Ront answered.

"And as Ront responds to you," Mr. R spoke up again. "You all feel the ground shake beneath you. Rolen, you begin to struggle to stay in the air."

"I come out of wild shape, landing myself onto the spire," Rolen said.

"As the dragon shifts back into its half-elven form, the bowl at the top of the obelisk begins to spin and change from blue to goldish yellow. With another blast of light, a beam of gold energy blasts into the sky, illuminating the dark sky," Mr. R continued. "In your arms, Ront, the now cold body of Froug begins to blow away into dust."

"He that dies pays all debts," Ront recited.

"Ooo, The Tempest. I love it!" Jake smiled.

"As the beacon of light intensifies, many beings in the army began to collapse and turn into dust as well. Those who were decayed and falling apart begin to rapidly decay at your feet. Those who seem unaffected, either panic and run from the scene or stand in awe at the bright beacon above." He clicked his keyboard.

On the screen was an image of the spire. Much like Mordor in Lord of the Rings. But less fire and eyes, and more light beam shooting into the sky.

"The beacon suddenly opens at the base. And through the opening steps an ethereal-looking gnome, a bright light illuminating and defining their outline. As the gnome comes closer into the material world. You recognize the face. There, standing in the beacon of light, is Froug. And as you all piece together who the being is, another creature walks up behind him. You instantly recognize this creature."

"Gerbo!" I blurted out.

"You all have done this world a grand service," Froug began. "Although it didn't seem as easy. You six have brought down Death's Hand. You have stopped Greg from becoming an undead monster. And you have brought me home."

"So what happens now?" Lerissa asked.

"I must take him with me," Froug answered. "Where we can finally pass on to the next life. Where after thousands of years, my brother and I can finally learn what it feels like to have lived."

Tears began to trail down my cheeks and I could feel my nose beginning to run. "But what about Gerbo?" I choked out.

"He has been in this world for as long as I have. His time comes with mine. However, I know of a hovel far in the west where owlbears are breeding like mice. I'm sure you can visit there and make friends with the owlbears. Maybe even one day have your own companion." Froug changed his smile into a weird frown of joy. "Now it is time that I take my brother. We haven't much time. And Froug reaches out for Greg who is still aimlessly floating around. When they make contact with each other, there is a glimmer of gold arcane energy that swirls around them, much like a Disney movie transformation. And the frail, old, and decrepit man suddenly becomes a young gnome man," Mr. R depicted. "F—Froug?" he stammered. "N— no! You can't! I won't!" He began to argue with himself.

Mr. R rolled a couple times. "And you all watch as Froug's expression grows from happy relief to painful sorrow."

"What's happening?" Rolen jumped.

"Brother, you must! We have nothing left in this world!" Froug looked worried. "No! With you gone, I have everything!" Greg hissed at himself. "You all watch as Greg's left eye begins to morph back into the misty green it had been. A nasty smile curls across his face. Goodbye, Froug. Enjoy eternity in the empty void of death!" He rolled one more time. "And with that, Greg shoves Froug back through the beacon and then disappears in a blast of black smoke."

"Son of a—" Ront blurted.

"The beacon closes, the light retreating back into the bowl. You all stand there alone in the Southland Ruins," Mr. R described. "Torinn and Ront, you still remain on the battlefield that now lays barren."

"Do we know what just happened?" Torinn asked.

"I'd say you both saw the beacon, a figure come out, and the beacon close," Mr. R answered.

Ront cupped his hands around his mouth. "What'd we miss?"

I turned to Ront and cupping my hands around my mouth. "Well, we did it—but we also didn't?"

"What does that mean?" Torinn joined in.

"Ugh." Lerissa groaned. "Can we move to a better talking location?"

"Sure, you four find your way down the spire where Torinn and Ront meet you at the bottom." Mr. R nodded.

"Okay, so what happened?" Ront asked again.

"So somehow Froug died, became ethereal—" Lerissa stopped as Torinn gazed at Ront. "I'm guessing you did something?" she scolded.

"He asked us to kill him," Ront defended. "I was fulfilling an already dying man's wish."

"Never mind." Lerissa shook it off. "Froug came through the beacon to take Greg into the afterlife. But—Greg had other ideas."

"What does that mean?" Torinn pried.

"He shoved Froug back into the beacon," I blurted out. "And then poof! He was just—gone."

"What do you mean, gone?" Ront raised his voice.

"Was that not obvious by poof?" Rolen shot back.

"So he's gone, Froug's dead, and we have no idea what to do next?" Ront listed off.

"Yup, looks that way." I frowned.

"So what the hell do we do now?" Rolen asked.

"Well, there still stands the question..." Gimble interjected. "Weren't Elfi and the others here?"

"Oh shi—" Rolen caught himself. "I race back up to find them!"

"As you climb back to the top of the massive spire—and I assume everyone follows—you crest to the top and find a dragonborn woman huddling around two dragonborn children," Mr. R said.

"No!" Rolen sighed.

"Where're the others?" Ront questioned. "Where's Elfi? The other kid?" He swallowed the knot in his throat. "Where's Jarron?"

"Akura!" Torinn jumped over Ront's grief. "Perra! Sora!"

"Torinn," Mr. R answered.

"Oh thank Pelor you three are safe!" Torinn sighed in relief. "Did they hurt you? Tell me you're okay."

"Through teary eyes, all three of them show you their forearms," Mr. R said, turning his arm over and pulling up his sleeve. He reached under the table and pulled out a red marker. He took the cap off with his teeth and moved to write on his arm.

Abomination

"You find this word carved into each of their arms. The wounds now scabbed and fresh scar tissue already formed."

"D—did they do this to you?" Torinn stuttered.

Mr. R nodded.

"I kneel down to look eye-to-eye with the girls, a hand on each shoulder. I promise you, each of you, that I will find him. I will make him pay for the sins he has committed not only against this world but against our family. I want you to remember what they thought about us. That word in your arm." He inclined his head at Mr. R's arm. "It shall never define us. Never! And I cast cure wounds on all three of them. Healing and erasing the scars." Torinn adjusted his hearing aid. "And when I find him, I will remind him of the pain and suffering he caused our family! Now let's get you three home. Kriv has to be worried sick about us."

"I want to pull Torinn aside after he gets back up," Ront said.

"What is it?" Torinn asked.

"We need to ask them if they know what happened to the others," Ront answered.

"In time, my friend. In time." Torinn reached a hand out and placed it on Ront's. "But for now, we need to let wounds heal. There are only so many wounds magic can heal. I understand you're desperate to find him, and I understand your pain.

But for now, we need to take this victory. Small it might be. Take this one and enjoy it. For we will never know when the next one will be. Or if it will be. But after some healing, I promise you as well, we will find them, and we will seek out retribution!"

"I'm holding you to that," Ront choked out. Tears welling in his eyes. "We should hurry and get them home. I could also use a drink or two after this journey."

"Me too!" I added. "So Lerissa, what do you say? Bamf us back to Dracomear for a drink?"

"You want to—" Lerissa caught herself. The anger draining from her face. "No, no, you guys are right. It's been a while since we rested. We will need to return to our mission right after," she said sternly.

"Agreed," we all said together. We all gathered hands and looked to Lerissa.

"To Dracomear," she said.

"And with that, you all get that familiar rushing sensation of teleporting," Mr. R began describing. "And when you feel the sudden stop, you all find yourselves inside a familiar cathedral with white marble pillars and floors with gold trim. Standing at the front resides a massive statue. You all recognize this as Torinn's temple to Pelor. And before anyone can so much as move you hear a voice echo through the hall. *You're Alive!* And when you all turn to see where the voice came from, a healthy and heavily armored Kriv comes running at you all. Ending his run scooping all the girls in his arms."

"I brought them home just as I promised." Torinn smiled. "They're safe now."

"As the family reconnects and shares a tearful reunion. The rest of you head out the temple doors and off to the tavern down the road," Mr. R began.

"I eventually catch up with them," Torinn added.

"Torinn eventually catching up with you all before you walk into the tavern. When you come inside, taking a seat at your usual table at this tavern you frequent in Dracomear, all eyes shift to you six." Mr. R smiled. "And that's where we will leave off for tonight."

THIRTEEN
MOVING FORWARD

WE ALL LET OUT A MASSIVE SIGH AND SAT THERE. NOBODY said a word for a good five, maybe even ten minutes. And then Liam broke the silence.

"So... that's it?" He threw his hands up. "We still need to chase him around?"

"I guess." I shrugged. "What more can we do?"

"But we've spent forever trying to find him!" Daryl added. "And we had him! How could we have lost him so easily?"

"You guys need to remember he's supposed to be a powerful being. Of course he escaped," Laura reminded us. "This is going to be a lot harder than we anticipated. But next time, we kill him. No matter what."

"Agreed," Jake nodded.

We all turned and looked at Ben. He was sitting there with his arms crossed, leaning back in his chair. Silent.

"You alright?" I asked him.

He nodded. He looked like he was deep in thought. Then he sat forward, landing his chair on all fours. He sifted through all of his papers and notes. "Who has the map?" he finally asked.

"I—I do?" Laura answered raising her eyebrow. She flipped to the back of her binder and pulled out a thick square of folded paper that she handed to her brother.

"Clear the table," Ben instructed.

We all followed his instructions and cleared our spots. He then proceeded to unfold the map onto the table. He ran his finger across the map, stopping his finger on the Southland Ruins. He then traced his finger up to Froug's home. The map read Port Saren. He then continued his finger east across the map to Allurena. Then moving east again to Faria and then further to Tal'ireald.

"Look at these," he told us.

"Those are the places we've been since this whole thing started. What about it?" Laura answered.

"It keeps going west. And each location has someone tied to Death's Hand. The contract guy in Tal'ireald. Reita in Faria. The temple and the guardian in Allurena. Heck, the guys who attacked us outside Dracomear. And then Froug in Port Saren. But then at the southernmost point of the map, we found Greg," Ben explained.

"So what?" Daryl asked. "We go to places chasing these kinds of people."

"Yeah, but look at the map again," Ben said. "Look at what each location has in common."

And there almost plain as day were temples at each of these towns and cities. Except in the Ruins.

"How did you see that?" Jake questioned.

"Well think about it. His ability derives from cheating the Raven Queen and Pelor, right? He's avoiding these temples. Hiding from the gods," Ben explained.

"So what you're saying is we need to drag him out towards a temple?" Liam pieced together.

"Maybe," Ben shrugged. "But that narrows down where we

can find him. We need to find the places that don't have a temple to either god. Track him down that way."

"So where do we start?" I asked.

"Let me take the map home with me and do some research on it. I'll bring a list of cities and towns that we should go through," Ben thought aloud. "I want to guess he's somewhere close to the Southlands. But he's also powerful..." He trailed off. "I'll come back with that list next week. We can start from there. Who knows, maybe one or two of these cities will have a side quest or something."

"I'll look into it with you," Laura said. "Maybe two sets of eyes will help."

"Text me the list and I'll do some in-game research since we're in Dracomear. That's also if we didn't completely ruin the library." Liam laughed, nudging Ben's shoulder.

"I'm little help on research." I threw my arm over Liam's shoulder. "But I'll come and help you get into the library. Stand guard and such if need be."

"Sure." Liam smiled. "That'd be cool. A little Adrik and Ront adventure."

"Well, what are we supposed to do?" Daryl asked wagging his finger between him and Jake.

"Come over and search the map with us," Ben answered. "Four sets of eyes are even better than two."

"Jake?" Daryl looked to his brother.

"Ya know, I wish I could. But I work all week. But you guys get together and do the search and send it to me. I've got the map on my computer anyways. Text me your list and I'll look at it when I work graveyard this week. Sound good?" Jake said.

"Works for me." Daryl shrugged.

"Can we come chill at Seven-Eleven with you and work with you?" Ben laughed.

"I wish," Jake chuckled. "But school first, remember."

"Lame," Ben sighed.

"I know." Jake shook his head smiling. "But it's gotta be done, right?"

"You guys are very determined on this." Mr. R smiled. "I'm glad you're all enjoying the story. Maybe I need to amp it up."

"No!" We all shouted.

"Let's finish off Greg before you go crazy. You've thrown ancient monsters at us before that are not meant to be killed." Daryl reminded him.

Mr. R chuckled. "I guess we'll see after all this research. You guys might be getting too smart for me." He turned his chair towards the kitchen doorway. "Now, you guys should get going. I don't want another call asking why some people haven't come home again." He raised his eyebrows looking at Laura, Ben, and I.

"I don't know what you're talking about." I smiled.

"It's not like we were doing anything," Laura defended. "These two losers couldn't stop trading pokémon until they had full pokédex. I just happened to be the one who had everything they needed."

"Well, either way, get home. It's already past curfew for a few of you." Mr. R shrugged and pointed to the clock on the opposite wall.

1:48

My phone started to buzz in my pocket.

<u>Mom</u>

-I'm leaving work now.
-Text me if you're done.

-I'll meet you for pie! :-)

-Just wrapped up!

-Be there in 15.

-Ok, Love you! <3

-Love you too!

"Alright, I guess I should go," I said looking up from my phone.

"Who are you talking to?" Laura asked.

I hadn't noticed it. But in the ten seconds, I had looked down to text my mom, everyone had left the room. I was in here alone with Laura. And that thought made my heart begin to race.

"Well?" Laura asked again.

"I—I" I stuttered.

"T—t—today junior," she joked. "I'm just giving you a hard time."

"O—oh." I laughed nervously. "S—so what're you up to tonight?" I went to lean on the chair next to me and missed the back. But I caught myself before falling like a fool.

"Well let's see, two am on a Saturday morning?" She stroked her chin as if there were a beard. Her eyes were no longer the reddish-yellow from before, but back to their normal beautiful color. "I might go do some major hardcore drugs. Rob a convenience store. Who knows, maybe kill a man." She grinned at me.

I must have looked frightened. And that must have amused her because she began to laugh. Like hardcore belly laugh.

"You didn't believe that did you?" she asked.

"Psh," I scoffed. "No way!" I threw my hands up as if to push away any thought of her killing anyone.

"Good," She shook her head. "No, I'll probably just go home and play some CS maybe watch some Netflix or Crunchyroll."

"Crunchyroll?" I looked at her puzzled.

"It's Netflix for anime. I've been sucked back into watching Naruto again. But I'm also rewatching The Office on Netflix again, so I really can't decide," she explained.

"Well here," I said, reaching for my d20 off the table. "Odds you watch anime. Evens, you watch The Office."

She bit her lip in contemplation. "But what if I don't like the outcome?"

"Well, it's not like you're contractually obligated to watch whatever the outcome is. But it will help you decide whether you want to watch this or you want to watch that." I held my hands out like scales. "So you ready?"

"Go for it." She smiled. "Oh wait, hang on." She put her finger up. "For good luck on the roll." And she leaned in and kissed my cheek.

I could feel my entire body begin to get warm and tingle. My fingers twitched, my knees wobbled, and my stomach did a flip. I went to speak, but nothing came out. I almost thought I was having another asthma attack. But I was still conscious. I shook my head to clear it.

"You alright?" Laura asked.

"Y—yeah. I'm great!" I assured her. I tried leaning on the chair again. This time I missed and fell to the floor. Knees were still jelly. I scrambled back to my feet and smiled at her as if nothing happened. "I—I'm sorry, what was I doing again?"

"You were rolling for me so I could see what I was gonna watch tonight." She laughed.

"Oh right," I remembered. I shook my fist for a minute or two before finally dropping the die on the table.

She smiled and picked up the d20 off the table and put it back in my hand. "Thanks, Jack." She hoisted her pack over her shoulder. She leaned down and kissed my cheek again before giving me a hug and walking into the kitchen.

I stood there for what felt like forever. But then my solitude was broken by a swift punch to the shoulder.

"Way to go. Two kisses this time and no asthma attack. You're becoming a man!" Liam smiled at me. "But you realize it still can't happen for quite a while right?"

"I know." I sighed. "But I heard at school from Katarina Markovski that state law is half your age plus seven—"

"You sound stupid, you know that?" Liam interrupted. "You sound like those losers in math trying to justify their actions. She's still too old for you and that's that."

I rolled my eyes. He was right and I knew it too. "Anyways, everyone left?" I asked.

"You think any of them can say goodbye?" Liam laughed. "You know how it is, one conversation leads to the next. That leads to some form of trading whether it's cards or video games." He stopped for a second and laughed at the floor. "Man, we're just a bunch of losers huh?"

"Wow, any more insults?" I said sarcastically slamming my hand to my chest dramatically.

"Your mother is a hamster?" He smiled.

"Well, your uncle smells of elderberries," I returned the expression. "I fart in thy general direction!" I continued, waving my hand from behind me.

My phone buzzed in my pocket again.

Mom
___

-I'm here.

-I'll be inside with a table for when you get here.

-Love you!

"Oh crap!" I blurted out. I moved to my stuff and began shoving everything into my bag.

"What?" Liam asked.

"My mom. She's down the street waiting for me to come get pie with her. She got out of work much faster than I thought she would."

"Well then, you need to get a move on!"

"No kidding!" I laughed. I struggled to zip my bag for a few moments, but once the bag closed, I threw my arms through the shoulder straps and proceeded into the kitchen.

"Hey, clueless," Liam called me. "Don't forget this!" He tossed a pink d20 at me. My pink d20.

"Oh man! Good catch!" I said as I caught the die. I hurried towards the front door where everyone stood in the way still chatting and everything.

"You off?" Mr. R asked me as I tried to get through the door.

"Yeah! Mom's down the street waiting for me to buy her some pie. I gotta hurry before they start thinking she's a pathetic crazy cat lady or something." I said, moving Daryl to the side of the doorway.

"Alright," Mr. R called to me. "Drive safe, okay? See you next week."

"I guess we'd better go too since we're in his way." Laura sighed. "Come on speed racer. I'm driving this time."

I heard everyone say their goodbyes as I got to my car and opened the door, but before I could get into my seat, an arm reached across and blocked me. I turned to see Laura.

"Here, this is yours by the way," She said handing me a card.

I turned it over to see it was a Red-eyes Black Dragon.

"I know Ben cheated it off you years ago. Finally managed to get it off him. Figured you'd want it back." She smiled at me. "I should let you go, your mom must be worried—"

I grabbed her jacket and pulled her in for a kiss. Every muscle in my body tensed and my face grew red hot with embarrassment. My knees began to wobble and I almost collapsed into her. I let her go and I could feel all life fade from my body as the blood rushed out of my cheeks and my face went cold. But I was sweating too. How was that a thing?

"I—I'm so sorry, Laura! I didn't mean to—I—I don't know what came over me," I stuttered trying to find a solid reason for why I did that. But to be honest, I had no reason. I just did it. Is that what love is? Having the urge to kiss your friend? I feel dirty for doing that. What if she didn't like that? Oh man, I could be in some deep shit!

"Bold move, cotton. Bold move." She smiled wiping her lower lip with her thumb. "I'll warn you, that may get you in some serious trouble with other people if you try that." She playfully punched my shoulder. "But you're safe for now. Just hope Ben didn't see that. Now go, your mom will be extra worried you're late if your excuse is because you were kissing me."

I smiled. "Again, sorry, it was an impulse. I shouldn't—"

She leaned in and kissed me again!

"Now shut up and go! I'll move so you can get out." She laughed as she walked away. She climbed into her car and her music blared from the stereo as the car roared to life. It was *Black Spider-Man* by Logic. The car made a clunking noise and drove back down the gravel path.

I finally regained control of my legs and climbed into my car. I started the engine and plugged the aux cord into my phone. I pulled up the Elton John album again and clicked play.

The song *Don't Go Breakin' My Heart* came on. I reached into my pocket and pulled out the picture of my parents I kept in my wallet, unfolded it, and stuck it on my dash display. I put the car in reverse and backed out of the drive.

ASSEMBLE THE PARTY

A SPECIAL PREVIEW

We hope that you liked this release from 5 Prince Publishing, LLC. Please enjoy the following excerpt from another book by this author, coming soon to 5PrinceBooks.com

TALES OF 1504 CEDARMEN DRIVE

BY ANTONY SOEHNER

IT WAS THE TYPICAL FRIDAY NIGHT DRIVE; FULL FOCUS ON the drive ahead and preparing myself for tonight's game. Rain spattered my windshield, but there wasn't quite enough rain falling to get my wipers wet. They squeaked across the semi-dry glass every time I pushed the bar up to set them off. Occasionally I had to pull it towards me to use the wiper fluid to get the glass wet enough to not ruin my blades.

The song *Let's Go Crazy* by Prince came on and I bobbed my head with the song's drum beat. This song always put me in a great mood, and lately, that mood had been sticking around.

Things were going pretty good for us! Mom had saved up enough money after being promoted at the bar, and dad's life insurance finally coming through, that she was able to negotiate a deal with the previous owners when they were selling the place. And now she is the proud owner of Travis' Bar. She managed to work the place into a more family-friendly venue in the past few months, and was able to hire Liam, Ben, Daryl, and I. She was able to even get Laura into some bartending classes and pulled her in with us in the kitchen as our head chef and weekend bartender. Jake swings by and helps us out every once and awhile when he's not working.

Mom created this business with our ragtag family of misfits, wackadoos, and whatchamacallits. Mr. R even comes by on nights Liam works and hangs out at the bar with Jake. It's become the new hang out for us.

But that hasn't changed our Friday night routine. We still all get together at Mr. R's house for game night. Mom has a whole Friday night staff. A group of employees who work throughout the week with us when mom schedules them. But they're all on the schedule for Friday nights so that the seven of us can play!

I took a deep breath, letting it fill my chest before slowly exhaling. "Adrik Frostbeard," I started to recite out loud. "Level sixteen dwarf barbarian. A hundred and seventy hit points. Nineteen strength," A smile grew across my face like it always did. "Ten charisma."

It had finally happened last week! We've been searching for weeks now since Greg disappeared. And I had just leveled up again. I finally got to move my charisma score to ten! I no longer had any negative modifiers. And boy did it feel great!

I pulled up in front of Liam's house, and of course, I was first. Wouldn't be right any other way. When I put my car in park and the song faded out, a car pulled up behind me with music blasting so loud I could hear the song as if I was playing it in my own car. It was *Enjoy the Rain* by Good Tiger, and that could only mean one thing.

"Laura!" I mumbled under my breath. I could already feel my legs wobbling and I hadn't even stood up yet. I began to struggle to breathe, like my seatbelt had tightened against my chest. I quickly unbuckled and opened my center console. I reached inside and grabbed my inhaler. I gave it a quick two puffs.

There was a knock on my window. I jumped, dropping my

inhaler on the floor. I turned to see Ben and Laura with their faces pressed against my window. Ben had his mouth open showing me his entire mouth. Laura had her nose flattened in a pig snout look. I rolled my eyes and smiled at the two. It's like they're related. I rolled down the window and they both backed up.

"Did we scare ya?" Ben asked. His eyes moving to the floor of my car.

I reached down and picked up my inhaler. "No," I lied. "You know my mom always wants me to bring this with me! I was just pulling it out to put in my bag."

"Whatever you say, wheezy," He mocked as he walked off towards the front door.

In response, I stuck my middle finger straight up. He shot me finger guns and continued walking.

"Ignore him," Laura laughed.

I turned to face her, and there was that beautiful complexion sitting in front of me. I sat there frozen in my seat. She was really close to my face. Like noses-almost-touching close.

I never know how to read these situations! I've spent years trying to figure women out. All these girls my age like to flirt and tell me about how great I'd be as a boyfriend, some even come hang out at my house and watch movies with me. But whenever I think about asking them out or asking what we are, they all freak out on me telling me I'm the same scumbag guy like the rest! But Laura was different. She didn't flirt around with me. Heck, we didn't hang out more than at work and on Fridays.

But seriously I think she might be the one! There's still that stupid age barrier though.

"You okay?" She asked.

I blinked back into reality. "W-what?" I stuttered. "Oh, yeah! Just got lost—"

"In my eyes?" She finished for me. "You need a better excuse, dude! You use that every time you zone out looking at me."

"I-I," I tried to answer, but I had nothing.

"It's cool," She laughed. "I know they're a soul-sucking pool! You don't have to be nice about it."

"Heh-heh," I fake laughed. I wasn't going to agree to that. She was perfect. Everything about her! Her smile that spreads to her gorgeous eyes! The Metallica tank top under the Star Wars replica jacket. The custom sneakers she'd painted with The Flash all over them. She was a walking billboard of geek! And I loved it!

"Jack?" She snapped her fingers in my face. "Dude, what is it? You okay today?"

"Yeah," I responded. "I just love you—" I caught myself. "Your presence!" I could feel my heart racing again. The blood rushing to my face. My eye's felt like they were bulging from my face. That was not slick at all! How stupid was I? How could you say that to her? You're not even dating! She's still too old for you! What the—

She leaned in and kissed my lips. I could feel my legs tense up in panic for a moment. She pulled away and chuckled.

"You're such a dork, Jack," She smiled at me. She tousled my hair. "Are you gonna be alright in there tonight? We have a world to save and I can't have you distracted!"

I nodded.

"Actually," I blurted out. What was I doing! This isn't going to work! Don't do it you, idiot! Don't do it!

But I did. I put my hand on her cheek and pulled her in for another kiss. A long one. My whole body felt like it melted in my seat.

Had that actually worked? Not only is she not pulling away, but she's kissing me back still.

"Oh good lord Pelor above!" A voice broke in.

I scrambled towards the origin of the voice to find Liam now sitting in my passenger seat.

"Would you two get a room, please?" He asked. He then proceeded to fake gag.

"Would you mind your own business?" I scolded him. "Laura and I were having a private conversation!"

"People usually talk with their tongues in their own mouths you know," He laughed as he swung out of the car, bouncing it as he did. "So whenever you two are done swapping spit. We'd love to have you inside!"

He ran back towards the house as I gave him the same gesture I gave Ben.

"Alright casanova," Laura smiled at me. "Let's go before they get suspicious."

I grabbed her jacket and pulled her in for one more quick kiss before she turned and walked towards the house.

What in the world just happened? Did I just make out with Laura? My dream girl? This has to be a dream! I reached down and pinched my leg.

Nope, not a dream. This was really happening! Laura is actually into me! Me! How was that possible? In every book and movie I've seen or read, the guy like me doesn't get the girl! It's not a thing!

I've dreamt that this would happen one day, but I couldn't have imagined it anytime soon. I'm always much older in my mind. Something of a rom-com kind of story; guy she's with breaks her heart, best friend and true love—me—swoops in, reminds her how amazing and beautiful she is, get married and grow old together, live a long, happy and geeky life together—

"Dude!" I heard Liam's voice again coming from my passenger side. Followed by a smack on the back side of my head.

"Ow!" I cried out.

"Seriously are you done gawking at her? She's not even standing there anymore." Liam reminded me.

"I wasn't gawking!" I lied. "I was getting in my pre-game headspace."

"No you weren't," He rolled his eyes. "You had that stupid smile on your face that you always get when you're daydreaming about your cheesy romantic comedy fantasy. The one where you and Laura grow old together."

"I don't know what you're talking about." I denied.

"Yes you do," He elbowed my side. "Where some guy breaks her heart, you swoop in and save—"

"Not a clue," I lied again.

"Whatever you say Mr. Sparks. Whatever you say." He closed the car door and walked back towards the house again. "Let's go!"

I finally killed the engine, unplugged my phone, and walked to the back of my car. I opened the back and grabbed my bag out. I threw it over my shoulder and closed my car. Clicking the key fob, it locked with a beep and I made my way inside. As I stepped into the house I could hear two more cars now pulling onto the gravel drive.

"Hey Liam," I shouted into the house. "Wade is here! You got the pizza money?"

"Don't worry about it!" I heard a voice call from outside. "We got it!"

I turned to see Daryl and Jake walking up the walkway with pizzas and a grocery bag.

"Wasn't Wade this time," Jake said. "New kid. Probably a week or two into working there."

"Is Wade okay?" I asked.

"Yeah, he said Wade's okay. Just running the shop tonight." Daryl answered.

I eyed him before reaching into my pocket and pulling my phone out. I clicked it open and went to my favorite contacts, clicking on the contact Pizza.

"What're you doing?" Daryl asked.

I held my finger up to him. The phone rang twice before a familiar voice answered.

"Kurtis' pizzeria and delicatessen, Wade speaking. How may I help you on this bodacious Friday evening?" Wade recited.

"Wade!" I said into the phone. "Hey, it's Jack!"

Before I could continue he spoke up, "Hey Jack-attack! What's going on my dude! Did y'all get your pizzas?"

"Yeah, we just did," I assured him. "I was calling to check and make sure everything was okay. The new guy said you were running the shop tonight."

"Oh yeah, I had to send out Tal tonight." He sighed. "Kurtis had a bit of a health scare yesterday. Ashley walked into the shop and found him passed out in the kitchen. Doc says he was overworking himself. Prescribed some medical stuff and some well-needed time off."

"But he's gonna be okay?" I asked.

"Oh for sure, bud," Wade chuckled. "He's a-okay! He came in a little bit ago to make sure you guys got your order in even!"

"Well, we're glad he's okay! Let him know we can't wait to hear from him when he's back."

"Will do ,my man! Will diddly do!" Wade sang. "You dudes have a fun night! Good luck on that Greg adventure!"

"Thanks, Wade, take it easy!" I told him.

"You too, Jack. Peace." The line went silent before the phone clicked telling me he hung up.

"So what's up?" Jake asked.

"Wade's running the shop tonight. Said Kurtis was told to take some time off. Doctor's orders." I explained.

"Well, as long as he's okay." Daryl sighed in relief.

"You said it!" Jake laughed. "That man's been throwing pizza since I was little. Couldn't imagine that place if he were gone."

"Well, let's not think about it," I said. "By the sounds of it, we won't have to worry about it for a while longer."

"Here's the money!" Liam ran into the room.

"You're too late," Jake chuckled. "We got it already."

"What?" Liam stood there in awe. "I didn't even get to say hi to Wade!"

"Well, none of us did," I shrugged. "He's running the store tonight while Kurtis is on doctor prescribed vacation."

"Is he okay?" Liam's eyes grew wider.

"He's fine," I explained again. "Just a little overworked. Doc told him he needed to take time off. So Wade is running the store."

"Well, as long as he's alright," Liam sighed.

"That's what I said!" Daryl smiled.

"Let's get these bad boys into the kitchen," Jake said patting the pizza boxes in his arms.

We all marched our way into the kitchen. And per usual with our group of friends, Laura and Ben had their gameboys out, connected between them with a semi-transparent cable.

"I've got Hitmonlee. Trade him for your Scyther?" Ben negotiated.

Laura swished her cheeks back and forth. "How about Hitmonlee for Jigglypuff? Or my Scyther for your Moltres. That would complete my legendary set."

"Hey!" Daryl interrupted the negotiation table. "Those are both mine!"

"It's just for Pokedex stats," Ben defended. "They'll go back to you. We're just trading around to complete our dex."

"Give you my second Mew to keep him," Laura smiled.

"Like I need another. I already have all of theirs," Daryl laughed as he gestured to the rest of us.

"So then why would you need either of these back?" Ben asked.

"Because I'm a perfectionist," Daryl smirked. "What's the point of being the very best if you don't have the very best?"

"I have no words." Laura scrunched her face.

"I battle you to win them back!" Ben challenged.

"You think that's going to go well for you?" Daryl folded his arms and shifted his weight to his back leg.

"I think it'd be worth the shot," Ben replied. He was chewing the inside of his cheek. A dead giveaway that he's nervous!

Daryl swung his bag around and opened it. He threw his hand deep into the bag before pulling out his own Gameboy.

"You really think you're ready for this?" Daryl asked.

Ben looked back at his Gameboy before looking back at Daryl. An ominous grin crossed his face. He said nothing and just nodded at Daryl. He offered him the other end of the cable that was connected to Laura's Gameboy.

I pushed my way around the dueling nitwits and grabbed myself a plate and some pizza. I scooted to the fridge and grabbed a root beer before heading into the game room out of all the chaos.

"Take that, son!" I heard Ben shout as I passed into the room.

I went to my seat and set my food on the table. I swung my bag off my back and placed it on the chair, then reached into my bag and pulled out my binder and player's handbook, setting them next to my plate. I reached back into my bag and pulled out my dice bag, and dropped it on my books with a thud and a rattle.

"Hey! Just the man I was looking for!"

I spun around to see Mr. R sitting in the doorway. He wheeled his way over to me and handed me a folded piece of paper.

"What's this?" I asked him. I could feel my eyebrow arching.

"Open it and see," He smiled at me, pushing the paper closer to me.

I took it from him and opened it. Inside was a picture. Mom in a hospital gown. In her arms was a baby. I was that baby. But behind my mother and I was a passed out dad in the hospital bed. And behind him, a standing, younger, Mr. R with a cup of water pouring out on my dad.

I couldn't help but let out a laugh. This was an amazing picture!

"Where did you get this?" I asked. The smile on my face never dropping.

"It was in a stash of Marisha's things I found in the basement." He said. You could see the physical battle in his face to avoid any outward sign of pain. "It was in the box of the undeveloped film she had. Figured it was time to sort through her things. I took her box of film to Walgreens and get them developed. This was the first picture I pulled out when I got home."

"Tell me you printed doubles?" I shook my head laughing. There was a knot forming in my throat. "You need to always have a copy of this picture!" I croaked out through the knot.

"Oh, I've got one. Don't you worry!" He assured me. "A genuine moment like this. I couldn't pass up my own copy!"

"Mom's gonna love this! Thanks, Mr. R," I leading over and gave him a hug. When I rested my chin on his shoulder, I caught a glimpse at a box sitting on the floor behind him. It was labeled—

Marisha's Things
Box 3 of 20

Sitting on top of the box were some cameras. There was a Polaroid camera sitting next to an older film camera. And next to that was a large professional digital camera.

"Are those her cameras?" I asked, standing back up and moving towards them to get a closer look.

"That's her collection." He sighed. "Her work camera, art camera, and spur of the moment camera. She sure did take a lot of pictures. That box could tell a bazillion stories."

I picked up the film camera and pulled the trigger to load the next frame. Turned to Mr. R and said, "Smile!"

The camera shuttered with a click. I pulled the trigger again and hung the camera around my neck.

"Do you mind if I use these tonight?"

"By all means kiddo!" He smiled. "They're all yours! She was your aunt after all!"

I couldn't believe it! After all these years... Aunt Marisha's cameras! They're mine! I also couldn't believe that he was willing to part with them. Ninety percent of these undeveloped film cartridges were probably of him.

"I have a feeling that wherever she and your dad are right now, they're smiling bright!" Mr. R said, choking through the tears now welling in his eyes.

"Now why don't we stop getting emotional over the past and go gather everyone together? Get this game a-rollin'."

MEET THE AUTHOR

Raised on a healthy diet of geek and pop culture, Antony has come to share his love and appreciation for role playing games and geek culture. If it's random comic book facts, Star Wars obsession, or just the measly obscure movie reference, Antony is there!

Walker Revenge Bernadette Marie
Lest We Aren't Forgiven *Railyn Stone*
Broken Hearts *M.O. Kenyan*
The Three Stones of Bethany *April Marcom*
Wanderlust *Bernadette Marie*